"Everything's status quo here. At least for the next ten days."

"What's happening in ten days?" she asked curiously.

"I have to take the boys to Las Vegas for the wedding."

"It makes sense that she'd want them there for her big day," Olivia noted.

"Maybe," he acknowledged. "But it also makes sense that she would have introduced them to the man who will be their stepfather before now, but that hasn't happened."

Olivia frowned. "They haven't met her fiancé?"

He shook his head.

"Well, that should be an interesting weekend for all of you," she mused.

"I can't wait," he said, rolling his eyes.

"Is there anything I can do to help?"

"You could be my date for the wedding."

Dear Reader,

I've always loved holiday romances. And single dad heroes. And marriage of convenience stories. (Yes, I'm a sucker for all the usual romance tropes!) So it was a lot of fun to put those elements together in a new Match Made in Haven story—with a little bit of "friends-to-lovers" and "second chances" thrown in, too.

Rancher Adam Morgan will do anything to keep his family together—even marry a woman he doesn't love. Because Olivia Gilmore is great with his kids, and that's more important than the unbidden attraction he feels for the sexy schoolteacher...isn't it?

Olivia is happy to step up when she learns that her best friend's brother is looking for a wife to help him maintain custody of his three sons. Because she adores Easton, Hudson and Colton—*not* because their dad was the object of her secret teenage crush.

Still, despite Adam's insistence that he's not going to fall in love again, Olivia can't help but hope that the time they spend together leading up to the holidays will change his mind—or even his heart.

I hope you enjoy *Countdown to Christmas* and look for more Match Made in Haven titles coming in 2023.

Happy holidays!

xo *Brenda*

Countdown
to Christmas

BRENDA HARLEN

HARLEQUIN

SPECIAL
EDITION

**HARLEQUIN®
SPECIAL
EDITION™**

Recycling programs
for this product may
not exist in your area.

ISBN-13: 978-1-335-72428-1

Countdown to Christmas

Copyright © 2022 by Brenda Harlen

For questions and comments about the quality of this book,
please contact us at CustomerService@Harlequin.com.

Harlequin Enterprises ULC
22 Adelaide St. West, 41st Floor
Toronto, Ontario M5H 4E3, Canada
www.Harlequin.com

Printed in U.S.A.

Brenda Harlen is a former attorney who once had the privilege of appearing before the Supreme Court of Canada. The practice of law taught her a lot about the world and reinforced her determination to become a writer—because in fiction, she could promise a happy ending! Now she is an award-winning, RITA® Award–nominated, nationally bestselling author of more than fifty titles for Harlequin. You can keep up-to-date with Brenda on Facebook and Twitter, or through her website, brendaharlen.com.

Books by Brenda Harlen

Harlequin Special Edition

Match Made in Haven

The Sheriff's Nine-Month Surprise
Her Seven-Day Fiancé
Six Weeks to Catch a Cowboy
Claiming the Cowboy's Heart
Double Duty for the Cowboy
One Night with the Cowboy
A Chance for the Rancher
The Marine's Road Home
Meet Me Under the Mistletoe
The Rancher's Promise
The Chef's Surprise Baby
Captivated by the Cowgirl
Countdown to Christmas

Montana Mavericks:
The Real Cowboys of Bronco Heights

Dreaming of a Christmas Cowboy

Montana Mavericks: What Happened to Beatrix?

A Cowboy's Christmas Carol

Visit the Author Profile page
at Harlequin.com for more titles.

For Virginia and Michael, who inspire me every day by living their real-life happily-ever-after.

(But especially for Virginia, who checks in every day to ensure I'm writing my fictional happily-ever-afters.)

Chapter One

His ex-wife was getting married.

Adam Morgan stared at the invitation in his hand, relieved to discover that the news of Rebecca's impending nuptials didn't elicit any strong feelings from him—or any feelings at all, really. Of course, almost five years had passed since she'd walked out on their marriage, leaving him and their three young sons.

Thankfully, they'd only been on their own for a few weeks before his mother took pity on them and moved in, because he honestly didn't know what he would have done without her. The arrangement had been good for Shirley Morgan, too. Helping care for her grandkids ensured that the recent widow, struggling to adjust to life without her husband of more than thirty years, was too busy to ever feel lonely.

And she was undoubtedly busy. In addition to taking over the grocery shopping, meal preparations and most other household chores, she also chauffeured the boys to various extracurricular activities, baked cupcakes for school events, supervised homework and played referee. She didn't hesitate to give any of the boys—including Adam—a stern talking-to if she felt it was needed, but her admonishments were always followed by hugs. And sometimes cookies.

A thought that had Adam eyeing the cookie jar hopefully, though he knew better than to look for a treat before he'd eaten his lunch. He tucked the invitation back into the envelope addressed to Adam Morgan & Guest, Easton, Hudson & Colton.

"When did you say Rebecca stopped by?" he asked his mom.

She turned the grilled cheese in the pan. "It was around two o'clock."

"Yesterday?"

"No. Today."

The clock on the stove read 12:58.

"How could she stop by around two when it's not yet one o'clock?" he asked.

His mother's cheeks were flushed—maybe from the heat of the stove or maybe from embarrassment. "I meant ten o'clock," she said now. "Rebecca was here at ten o'clock."

Which would explain why he hadn't seen her vehicle parked by the house, as he'd spent most of the morning at the far boundary of the property, checking the fence.

"If she'd waited until this afternoon to visit, she could have seen the boys," he remarked.

"You can't honestly be surprised that she didn't consider their schedule when she decided to drop by," Shirley chided, as she turned the sandwich onto a plate.

He wasn't surprised, but he was disappointed for his sons, who didn't see their mom nearly as often as they should.

"And yet she apparently expects them to be at her wedding," he noted.

"She does," Shirley confirmed, handing him the plated sandwich, neatly cut into two triangles, and began filling a bowl with soup.

"You do know I'm capable of making my own lunch, don't you?" he said. "There's no reason for you to cook for me every day."

"I like to keep busy," Shirley said. "And I don't like you making a mess of my kitchen."

"That's fair," he acknowledged, as he carried his grilled cheese to the table.

She set the bowl beside his plate.

"Aren't you eating?"

"I had a big breakfast."

"Five hours ago," he noted, lifting his sandwich to his mouth.

She took a seat across from him. "I haven't done much of anything in those five hours to work up an appetite."

"You should eat, anyway." He put the spoon in the bowl of soup and slid it toward her, then rose from the table to refill a second bowl.

"The ATV sounded a little rough this morning," Shirley noted, when he'd returned to the table.

"A cracked intake boot."

"Are you going to replace that before or after you repair the barn roof?"

"That's a good question," he acknowledged.

Because it had been one of those weeks, starting with the loss of two young calves taken down by coyotes, followed by the ruin of several bags of grain as a result of the previously undetected leak, and now the ATV.

The never-ending joys of being a rancher, he mused wryly.

All of that capped off by the unexpected invitation to his ex-wife's wedding.

"You should go," Shirley said, interrupting his musing.

"To fix the roof?"

"To the wedding," she clarified.

"I don't have much of a choice," he admitted. "Rebecca wants the boys to attend—and they should—and how else would they get there?"

"It will be good for you to get away," his mom said, ignoring his rhetorical question. "Maybe meet some new people."

It had become a familiar refrain in recent months, as she'd taken to reminding him that he was too young to be alone. And while it was true that he'd only turned thirty-five on his last birthday, he felt so much older than that number and too tired to engage in the usual dating games.

Sure, he missed sex. *A lot.* But when he considered the effort it would take to go out and meet someone that he liked well enough to get naked with, he decided it simply wasn't worth the trouble.

But Shirley's interest in his personal life wasn't the

only change he'd noticed in the past year—nor was it the most troubling one. Of far greater concern was her increasing forgetfulness and occasional confusion. As a result, he'd been searching for ways to ease her responsibilities, such as enlisting his sister to take the boys from school to their extracurricular activities so that their mom didn't have to drive into town, and offering to do the grocery shopping when he was picking up an order from the feed store.

Of course, Shirley usually declined that offer, wanting to pick her own produce and instruct the butcher on her preferences. So far, he'd acquiesced to most of her wishes, though he usually made an excuse to go into town at the same time, so that he could drive her to and from the store.

"Maybe," he finally responded to her remark.

But if he was going to take time away from the ranch, he would prefer to do so for fun. Rebecca Hollister as The Bride: Part Two was *not* his idea of fun.

"And it might be good for you, too," he added.

Shirley shook her head. "Even if I wanted to go, and I don't," she quickly assured him, "my sister is going to be here that weekend."

"You didn't tell me that Aunt Mary was coming for a visit."

"I'm sure I did."

But she didn't sound sure. And though Adam knew it was entirely possible that she had told him and he'd forgotten, it was more likely that she'd forgotten to tell him.

Either way, there went any hope of having his mom's

company—and an extra set of hands—on his road trip with the boys.

Unless he could sweet-talk his sister into going with them.

The usual after-dinner routine in the Morgan house involved helping to tidy up the kitchen, then completing any remaining homework, followed by bath time and story time. Tonight, thanks to his ex-wife's impending nuptials, Adam had one more task to add to their nightly schedule.

He called Easton and Hudson into the room where his youngest son was surveying the contents of his bookcase, his blanket tucked under one arm and Bruno—a plush dinosaur toy—dangling from his hand.

"Sit down," he instructed the older boys, gesturing to Colton's bed. "I need to talk to you about something."

Easton and Hudson exchanged worried glances as they perched cautiously on the edge of the mattress.

"It's not about Lollipop's stall door being left open," Adam told them.

The brothers shared another look.

"You know about that?" Hudson asked.

"You think I wouldn't notice that the horse was on the wrong side of the paddock fence?"

"So we're not in trouble?" Easton's tone was hopeful.

"I didn't say you weren't in trouble—I said this conversation isn't about that."

Colton, having finally selected a book, bypassed the bed to climb into his dad's lap, holding his blanket, toy and storybook now. He snuggled into Adam's chest and rubbed his cheek against his soft flannel shirt, just like he'd done when he was a baby.

Of course, he *was* still Adam's baby, but he was growing up fast. The day would come, probably far too soon, that the little boy didn't turn to his dad for comfort, but he was glad to know that time wasn't now.

"What's it about then?" Easton asked, wary again.

"Your mom's getting married."

The boys took a moment to consider this information.

Hudson was the first to speak, asking, "Who's she gonna marry? You?"

Adam responded quickly. "No."

Hell, no.

"The man's name is Greg Burnett."

"Oh." Hudson's hopeful expression faded. "I thought maybe we were gonna be a real family again."

And didn't those plaintive words arrow straight into his heart?

Because if there was one thing he'd always tried his damnedest to do, it was ensure that his sons didn't ever feel as if they were missing out on anything because their mom and dad didn't live together.

Obviously he'd failed.

Obviously an onsite grandmother and doting aunt couldn't compensate for the fact that their mother had been mostly absent from their lives for the last four and a half years.

"We *are* a real family," he said now, because he believed it was true. Maybe they weren't a traditional family, but they were as real as the pain he felt anytime one of his children was hurting.

"Clive says our family is broken."

"Our family is not broken," Adam said, even as his heart was cracking.

"But it's not fair," Hudson grumbled. "Hanna C has two moms and we don't even have one."

"You do have a mom," he reminded them.

Easton snorted. "Not a real mom."

Adam couldn't really dispute that point, but he felt compelled to speak up in Rebecca's defense, albeit more for the sake of his children than his ex-wife. "Your mom might not spend a lot of time with you, but I know she loves you."

"When she gets married, will this Greg guy be our new dad—like when Elliott's mom married Mr. Gilmore?" Hudson asked.

Jeez, they were killing him with these questions.

"He'll be your stepfather," Adam managed to respond evenly.

"Do we hafta caw him dad?" Colton asked, sounding troubled.

Please, no.

"That's entirely up to you," he told them.

"I say *no way*." Easton folded his arms over his chest. "Dad's our dad. This guy is just someone our mom wants to marry."

"No way," Hudson agreed, folding his arms, too.

"No way," Colton said, dutifully echoing his brothers' words and posture.

Their unflinching loyalty went a long way to soothing Adam's bruised heart.

"The wedding's next Saturday in Las Vegas," he told them. "And your mom wants you to be there."

"I don't wanna go," Easton said.

"I understand that you might feel uncomfortable, because there will probably be a lot of people you don't know, but I'll be there with you."

"You will?" His eldest son sounded skeptical.

"I will," he promised.

"I still don't wanna go," Easton said.

"Sometimes in life we have to do things that we don't think will be a lot of fun," Adam said. "And sometimes we're surprised to discover that they're more fun than we anticipated."

"What happens at a wedding?" Hudson asked.

"The bride and groom stand up in front of their families and friends and promise to love one another forever," Adam said, grateful to finally have an easy question to answer.

"Or until they decide to get divorced," Easton added, sounding far more cynical than any nine-year-old should.

Hudson looked troubled. "Do we hafta get dressed up for the wedding?"

Adam chuckled. "I'm sure your mom would appreciate it if you showed up looking your best."

"That means a tie, doesn't it?" Easton wrinkled his nose.

"It does, indeed," he confirmed.

His eldest son sighed wearily. "I *hate* wearing a tie."

"We'll suffer together," he promised.

He only wished that the dress code was his biggest concern.

When all the boys' questions had been answered and they were settled in their respective beds, Adam made his way back down the stairs and settled behind his desk in the den. He had some paperwork to review and materials to order to fix the barn roof before he could call it a night, but first he called his ex-wife.

"Congratulations," he said, when Rebecca answered the phone.

"You obviously got my invitation," she noted.

"I did," he confirmed.

"And you'll all be at the wedding?" she asked hopefully.

"We will," he promised. Because he wanted his children to have a good relationship with their mom and would do everything in his power to facilitate it.

"Great," she said. "I'll add four plates to our final tally for the caterer."

"Five," he said.

"I'm sorry?" Rebecca was obviously taken aback by his response.

"The invitation was to Mr. Adam Morgan *and guest*," he reminded her.

"Well, yes," she admitted. "But I didn't think… I mean, I didn't know you were seeing anyone."

"A few hours ago, I didn't know you were getting married again."

"Fine," she finally replied. "The tables seat eight, anyway, so I'll make sure there's a place for you and—" she paused then, and he could envision her tapping a painted fingernail against her chin "—should the place card read *Jamie* or *Shirley*?"

The implication, of course, being that he didn't actually have a date but would drag his sister or his mom along to keep him company.

And *dammit*, that *had* been his intention. But no way was he going to admit that to his ex-wife now.

"It can simply read *guest*," he said instead.

"Well, I'll look forward to meeting your...*guest* at the rehearsal dinner."

Which meant that Adam had eleven days to snag a date or he'd be eating crow.

Chapter Two

Olivia Gilmore hadn't always dreamed of being a second-grade teacher. As a child, whenever she was asked what she wanted to be when she grew up, she rarely gave the same answer twice. Her earliest memory was of aspiring to be a ballerina, because she couldn't imagine anything more wonderful than dancing every day. Sometime after that, she decided that her future was with the postal service, because everyone loved getting mail. After a fire drill at school, she considered being a firefighter, because they were real-life heroes. Then she decided that if she was going to be a hero, she might as well be Wonder Woman, wearing those shiny bracelets and wielding the lasso of truth.

Sure, she enjoyed playing school, setting up her dolls and other stuffed animals and pretending to teach them the same things she'd learned in class that day. But she also liked to play baker, cooking up delicious snacks in her Easy-Bake Oven. And even if her creations weren't as fancy as some of the cakes on the baking programs her mom watched on TV, she had no doubt that she would be able to create equivalent masterpieces if her mom would let her loose in the kitchen. And sometimes she took a turn at being a crime-scene investigator, scouring the house with her magnifying glass, looking for clues to determine who had dropped a dirty sock in the hall—the culprit was inevitably one of MG or Mitchell, her annoying older brothers; who didn't put the cap back on the toothpaste—again, MG or Mitchell; and who stole her Halloween candy—in that case, it was MG *and* Mitchell.

It wasn't until high school that, at the behest of her guidance counselor, she seriously put her mind to consideration of a future career. But even then, she was less concerned about a potential job than her vocation—which she felt certain was to be a mother. And she didn't need to go to school to learn those skills, because she had two amazing role models in Angela Gilmore, her own mom, and Shirley Morgan, her best friend's mother.

But when she completed the aptitude tests she was given, her responses suggested a career as an occupational therapist, a midwife, school or career counselor (she got a chuckle out of that one) or teacher. And suddenly she remembered how much she'd enjoyed all the hours she'd spent "teaching" her dolls.

Teaching was also, in her opinion, the perfect occupation for a woman who wanted, more than anything, to be a mom, because when she finally had children, she'd have the same holidays from school that they did. In the meantime, she'd get to spend her days surrounded by other people's little ones, not only imparting her knowledge but also—and more important—nurturing their hopes and dreams.

She truly did love her job and (almost) all of the children who passed through her classroom. If she had any cause for disappointment about her life choices, it was simply that her thirtieth birthday was on the horizon and she had no prospects for a husband or a family. And it wasn't for lack of trying.

In the past fifteen months, since her brother Mitchell had finally married Lindsay Thomas, making her parents, Angela and Charles, instant grandparents to Elliott and Avenlea, Lindsay's son and daughter from her first marriage, Angela had been hinting—with all the subtlety of a bulldozer—that she couldn't wait for her other two children to settle down and give her more grandbabies to spoil.

Olivia had dutifully gone out with every single man that her mother had thrown in her direction—and several that she'd crossed paths with on her own—because she wanted to fall in love, marry and have a family. But none of the men she'd dated had made her aspire to even a second outing, never mind a lifetime together.

So for now, she was focusing all her time and attention on the nineteen second-graders in her class, because she did love being a teacher. And she loved how her students were like thirsty little sponges, eagerly absorbing everything she taught them. Most of the time, anyway.

This whole week, they'd been bouncing off the walls—because it was early in November and they were undoubtedly still making their way through their Halloween candy. Based on her experience, they would start to come down from the sugar high just in time to get wound up for the Thanksgiving holiday…and then Christmas.

"Clive, have you finished your work already?"

The curly-haired boy quickly swiveled in his seat, turning away from the friend who sat behind him to face the paper on his desk. "Almost," he said.

"*Almost* doesn't get you outside at recess, does it?"

"No, ma'am."

"Addison. Isabelle."

The twins glanced up, wearing identical guilty expressions on their faces.

"This isn't group work," she reminded them.

They reluctantly moved apart.

Elliott Gilmore, her brother's stepson, was counting on his fingers. Hudson Morgan, her best friend's nephew—and one of her nephew's best friends—was staring intently at his paper. Omar Chason—the third musketeer in the close-knit group of friends—was chewing on the end of his pencil, but his gaze was focused on the window. Omar had a tendency to daydream, but only after his work was done. Undoubtedly the star of her class, but one who didn't like to show others how brightly he could shine.

"If your worksheet is complete, and you've double-checked your work, you can read quietly or choose a coloring page from the art box."

Omar pulled a book out of his desk. While a lot of his friends were still reading graphic novels, he was already following the exploits of a young Harry Potter.

"Miss Gilmore! Miss Gilmore! I'm done!"

That was Scotty, waving his arm in the air.

Of course he was finished. He was always one of the first to complete any assignment. Unfortunately, he was sometimes more intent on getting done than doing things correctly.

"Bring your paper up," she suggested.

She spent the next twenty minutes reviewing the papers of other students as they finished the assignment, gave out two hall passes for bathroom breaks and refereed a dispute over what was apparently the last red crayon in the communal crayon basket.

When the bell finally rang, not just ending the period but signaling recess, she was almost as relieved as her students that they were able to go outside to run around and hopefully burn off some of their excess energy.

"Boots, coats, hats, mittens," she reminded them, as they beelined toward their cubbies.

She exhaled a quiet sigh of relief when they exited, en masse, then frowned when she discovered that one of her students had remained behind.

"Hudson, it's recess."

"I know," he said.

She took a few steps closer to his desk and saw that he was drawing a picture in his journal. Though he sometimes grumbled about art class, he was a creative child, often doodling in his free time.

"Don't you want to go outside and play with your friends?" she prompted.

"I wanna finish this," he said.

"You can take it home to finish it," she told him.

Because it was school policy that kids were expected

to be outside on the playground at both morning and afternoon recesses and on their lunch break, where they would be supervised by the staff members on duty and so that the other teachers could prepare for their upcoming lessons. Not that Olivia usually minded when one or more of her students wanted to hang out in the classroom. Despite her warning to Clive, she rarely kept any of them inside to finish work, because she believed it was important for them—and the class as a whole—to get fresh air and exercise.

So while she didn't mind that Hudson wanted to stay in, she was a little concerned. He was usually at the front of the line to go outside, to play whatever game his friends were playing and burn off some of the energy second-graders seemed to have in abundance.

"I'll bet Elliott and Omar are wondering where you are," she said gently.

"Nah," he denied. "I told them that I was going to stay in."

She sat sideways on the seat of the adjacent desk, facing him. "Why don't you tell me why you'd rather stay inside than be with your friends?" she suggested.

"'Cuz I wanna finish my picture," he said again. He looked up from his page then, his green eyes hopeful. The moss color was a Morgan trait, shared by each of his brothers, his aunt—Olivia's best friend—and his dad. "Can I stay in? Please?"

How could she possibly say no to such a polite and plaintive request?

"Okay, then," she agreed. "But just this once."

He rewarded her with a shy smile that only hinted at the heartbreaker she had no doubt he'd grow up to be.

Just like his dad.

She'd been fifteen when her hormones had woken up and suddenly realized that her BFF's older brother was incredibly good-looking. Prior to that, he'd simply been an annoying and obnoxious older sibling, and since Olivia had two of those of her own at home, she hadn't really paid him much attention.

Thankfully, he'd never known that one of the many girls who'd sighed over him was his sister's best friend. Not only because she would have felt humiliated if he'd known about her crush, but especially because, ten years later, Easton, his firstborn son, had been one of her students. And now Hudson, his middle child, was in her class. And in another two years, Colton, his youngest, would follow.

The bell rang again, summoning students back to class, and the remainder of the afternoon passed uneventfully. At the end of the day, after everyone else had gone, she tidied up her desk, then went to check the cloak room. In warmer weather, it wasn't unusual for students to forget hats and mittens—or even their coats sometimes. But colder temperatures had already fallen upon northern Nevada, ensuring that none of them ventured out without being properly bundled up. A bigger concern to Olivia was the possibility of leftover food: half-eaten sandwiches and trampled cookies and dripping juice boxes, any of which could draw insects and rodents.

She swept up cracker crumbs, tossed candy wrappers in the trash...and sighed when she discovered an abandoned backpack.

She usually did a quick visual check as her class filed out the door, but Peyton Nash had been near tears when the bell rang, struggling to fit her snow pants in her bag, and Olivia had been so focused on helping that half her students had gone before she'd realized that the line was moving.

The tag hanging from the zipper identified the owner of the backpack as Hudson. Though Olivia believed that students needed to learn to be responsible for their own belongings, she decided that delivering the forgotten bag to Morgan's Glen would give her the opportunity to talk to Adam.

Only because she was concerned about the boy's out-of-character behavior earlier that day—not because her foolish heart still nurtured the remnants of a long-ago crush on the boy's dad.

Adam was in the barn when an apple-green Hyundai pulled into his driveway and parked behind his mom's Jeep Cherokee. Zipping up his jacket in deference to the cold, he headed outside to greet his unexpected visitor.

"Miss Gilmore," he said, his surprise quickly followed by apprehension when he recognized his sister's longtime BFF—who also happened to be his middle son's second-grade teacher.

"We're not in the classroom now," she pointed out. "You can call me Olivia."

"Of course." He scrubbed a hand over his unshaven jaw. "Habit, I guess. All I heard when Easton was in your class two years ago was 'Miss Gilmore this' and 'Miss

Gilmore that,' and since September, it's been the same thing from Hudson."

She smiled with pleasure as she took a few steps closer. "It's always nice for a teacher to know that she's making an impression on her students."

"Are you kidding?" Adam said. "Hudson can't wait to go to school every morning. He hates weekends, because chores around the ranch are boring but Miss Gilmore's class is fun."

"And educational," she assured him. "But I try to keep the emphasis on fun, so they don't balk at learning."

"Well, whatever you're doing, it works," he told her.

Her lips curved again. "Good to know."

"But I don't know why you're here—did I forget a parent-teacher conference?" he asked. Although the puffy coat she wore covered her from chin to knees, the charcoal-colored pants and low-heeled black boots suggested that she'd come directly from school.

"No." She held up a familiar backpack. "But Hudson forgot this."

"And you drove all the way out here to drop it off?" He was grateful, but still a little wary. None of his boys had ever gotten into serious trouble at school, but he'd never had one of their teachers show up on his doorstep, either.

"It was on my way."

His eyebrows lifted. "Don't you live in town?"

He was certain that she did, because he recalled Jamie mentioning that her friend had a town house in the same neighborhood when he'd been helping his sister move.

"I do," she confirmed. "But I usually go to the Circle

G on Wednesdays—to exercise Dolly and have dinner with my parents."

"Dolly?"

Her cheeks flushed. "A lot of my parents' horses are named after country music icons. Kenny, Dolly, Reba."

Looking at her now, it was easy to forget that she'd grown up on a ranch. In fact, the Circle G—owned by her father and his brothers—was the biggest (and undoubtedly most profitable) cattle ranch in northern Nevada. But Olivia had never acted spoiled or entitled and, honestly, of all his sister's friends, she was the one he'd always thought the least annoying.

But it wasn't until he'd walked into her classroom at Stoney Ridge Elementary for his first parent-teacher interview when Easton was in second grade that he realized his little sister's friend was all grown up—and undeniably attractive. Five feet seven inches tall (two inches taller than his sister, who frequently grumbled about her height) with subtle but undeniably feminine curves, dark curly hair, even darker eyes fringed by thick lashes and temptingly shaped lips that were quick to smile.

He tore his gaze away from those lips now, because he had no business thinking of his son's teacher as an attractive woman. And even if she wasn't Hudson's teacher, she was Jamie's best friend, which meant that she was definitely off-limits to him.

"Well, I appreciate you dropping off the backpack," he said, attempting to nudge her along.

"Actually, if you've got a minute, there was something

else I wanted to talk to you about," Olivia said, clearly unwilling to be nudged.

"About Hudson?" he guessed.

She nodded.

"So this *is* a parent-teacher conference."

"No," she denied. "It's simply a teacher having a casual conversation with a parent about a student."

"What did he do?" Adam asked. "Besides forgetting his backpack, I mean."

"It's more what he *didn't* do," Olivia told him. "He didn't want to go outside for recess today."

He frowned. "That doesn't sound like my son."

"It surprised me, too," she said.

"Did he say why?"

"He said he wanted to work on the illustrations for a story he's writing in his journal."

Adam was stunned. "You're telling me that he gave up the chance to run around outside to do homework?"

"And now you know why I was concerned."

"Did he have a fight with Elliott or Omar?"

"I don't think so. I let the kids pick their own groups for a last-period science activity, and the three of them gravitated toward one another, as they always do."

"Do you think I should ask him about it?"

"That's entirely up to you," she said. "It was only one day—and one recess—but then when he forgot his backpack, I wondered if there was something going on at home that was causing him to be distracted."

He shook his head. "Everything's status quo here. At least for the next ten days."

"What's happening in ten days?" she asked curiously.

"Their mom's getting married again."

"Maybe that's why Hudson seemed a little preoccupied today." She looked at him, sympathy and concern in those big brown eyes. "Are *you* okay?"

"Me?" He was surprised that she would ask. "I'm fine. Except that I have to take the boys to Las Vegas for the wedding."

"It makes sense that she'd want them there for her big day," Olivia noted.

"Maybe," he acknowledged. "But it also makes sense that she would have introduced them to the man who will be their stepfather before now, but that hasn't happened."

Olivia frowned. "They haven't met her fiancé?"

He shook his head.

"Well, that should be an interesting weekend for all of you," she mused.

"I can't wait," he said.

"Is there anything I can do to help?"

"You could be my date for the wedding."

Olivia blinked. "Oh… Um…"

"I was kidding," Adam quickly assured her.

"Oh." She managed a weak smile. "Of course."

Did she sound just a little bit disappointed?

The possibility was…intriguing.

"Although…I don't yet have a plus-one," he confided.

"You have something even better," she noted. "Plus-three."

"Which will only make it that much harder to finagle a date," he lamented. "And I'm working on a tight schedule."

"I'm sure you'll figure something out."

Adam wasn't nearly as optimistic. But while the

prospect of taking Olivia to the wedding had snagged his attention momentarily, he had enough going on in his life without adding the complication of an unexpected attraction to the mix.

Chapter Three

After Olivia had gone, Adam finished feeding the horses and shut them in for the night. Though it was only early November, the nights were already bitterly cold and he worried that it was going to be a long, hard winter. Of course, being a rancher, he was preoccupied with the weather and constantly worried about how it would affect the land, the crops and the animals. Morgan's Glen had been operating in the black for the past several years, but he knew from experience that one bad season could change everything.

Shaking off his worries, he carried Hudson's backpack into the house and left it by his coat in the mudroom, where the boys dropped their outerwear when they got home from school.

And *dropped* was an accurate description, though

their grandmother usually marched them back to hang their coats and snow pants on the hooks he'd installed so the garments would be dry when they needed them again the next morning.

"Mmm…something smells good," he said to his mom, as he made his way to the kitchen sink to wash up for dinner.

"Chili," she said, stirring the stew in the pot on the stove. "I figured it would warm you up after such a cold day."

"It was cold out there," he agreed.

"And busy," she noted.

Of course, the kitchen window overlooked the driveway, ensuring that she had a clear view of anyone coming or going when she was in the kitchen—which was most of the time.

He nodded. "I'll fill you in on the details later."

"If you want," she said, suggesting that she had no intention of prying when they both knew otherwise.

"Why do I only see two lunchboxes on the counter?" Adam asked, as he joined his boys at the table, where they were doing their homework.

At least Easton seemed to be doing homework, while his younger brothers were playing some kind of video game on their handheld systems.

"I forgot mine at school," Hudson admitted, without glancing up from his screen.

"Just your lunchbox? Or your backpack with your lunchbox in it?"

"My backpack," he confirmed.

"Did you have any homework?" Adam pressed.

"I'm s'posed to read a chapter in my library book."

"And where's the book?"

"In my backpack," Hudson confided.

"Then I guess it's a good thing Miss Gilmore dropped it off."

Hudson finally looked up from his game, his eyes growing wide. "Miss Gilmore was here?"

Adam nodded. "She was going to her parents' house, and our house was on her way. But don't count on her doing it again," he cautioned. "You have to be more responsible with your things, kiddo."

"I will," Hudson promised.

"Good." Adam nodded then turned his attention to his youngest son. "And why aren't you doing homework?"

Colton giggled. "'Cuz I'm in kinda-gah-ten."

"I had homework in kindergarten," Easton chimed in. "Because cranky Mrs. Enbridge was my teacher."

"What have I told you about being respectful of other people?" Adam asked.

"To be respectful of other people," Easton echoed.

"And respectfully, Mrs. Enbridge was a grumpy old woman who should have retired ten years ago," Shirley said.

"Not helping, Mom."

A smile tugged at Easton's lips.

"I had Mrs. Enbridge, too," Hudson reminded them all. "And I agree with Gramma."

"I wike Missus Gi-mow," Colton said now. "She tells us sto-wees an' teaches us songs an' we get to paint wif our fin-duhs."

"It sounds like kindergarten is the place to be," Adam mused.

Hudson's brow furrowed, as if he was only realizing now that Colton's teacher had the same last name as his teacher. "Are Missus Gilmore and Miss Gilmore sisters?"

"No," Adam said. "They're cousins by marriage."

"What does that mean?"

"Missus Gilmore—Colton's teacher—used to be Miss Channing, but then she married Caleb Gilmore, who is Miss Gilmore's cousin," he explained.

"Why are there so many Gilmores?" Hudson asked.

"Because they have a big family."

"The Gilmores were also one of the founding families of Haven," Easton said. "We learned about that in social studies last year."

"Whatsa found fam-lee?" Colton wanted to know.

"Founding family," Easton said again, enunciating clearly for his little brother. "It means they were the first people to live in this area. Well, the Gilmores and the Blakes."

"Look at that," Adam mused. "My son is actually paying attention and learning something in school."

"I like history," Easton said.

"How about chili?" Shirley asked. "Do you like chili? Because I'm ready to dish up dinner, but the table is covered with books and papers."

The boys quickly cleared the space, then counted out cutlery and napkins and set them around the table while Adam sliced the loaf of crusty bread his mom had made while she ladled the spicy stew into five bowls.

It was all a familiar and comfortable part of their daily routine, and as they sat down to dinner, Adam said a silent prayer of thanks for his family—the reason for everything that he did.

Olivia was at Morgan's Glen longer than she'd intended, which meant that she didn't have as much time with Dolly as she'd hoped. Still, she made sure that the old mare got a decent workout, and as they galloped over the fields, she felt her worries melt away like morning dew under the sun's rays.

She loved living in town. Not just because it made her daily commute to school so much easier, but because living on her own afforded her a degree of freedom and independence that she wouldn't have if she was still at the Circle G. Though her parents made an effort to acknowledge that she was a grown woman, they still tended to be a little overprotective of their only daughter.

After she'd cooled down and groomed the horse, she made her way to the house. She gave a perfunctory knock on the door, then pulled it open and stepped inside the vestibule. She sniffed the air, recognizing the scents of homemade tomato sauce, spicy sausage and tangy oregano.

Lasagna, she guessed, as her stomach growled with impatience, reminding her that lunch had been a long time ago.

She removed her coat and boots, then immediately moved to the sink to pump soap onto her hands to wash up in preparation for dinner.

"You're late," Angela Gilmore chided, as she opened the oven to remove the tray of pasta.

"Better late than pregnant," she said lightly.

Her mother did not look amused by her flippant response.

"I'd be happy to hear that you were having a baby—especially if you'd met a nice man who'd put a ring on your finger."

"That's a change," Olivia noted. "You usually say, *but only after* you've met a nice man, et cetera."

Her mother shrugged. "Considering that you're almost thirty years old, I've decided that maybe I need to stop being so particular. Or maybe you do."

"Thirty isn't old," she said, though she was already feeling as if her window of opportunity to meet a wonderful man, fall in love, get married and have the two or three kids she'd always longed for was closing.

"I'd been married five years and was pregnant with my second child by the time I was thirty," Angela reminded her.

"Yeah, but that was fifty years ago," Olivia teased.

"It was thirty-three years ago."

"I know." She kissed her mother's cheek. "Just as I know that Dad loves you even more today than the day he married you."

"Because I have the evening meal on the table promptly at six o'clock every night."

"He's not going to stop loving you because you're serving up dinner at six-oh-four."

"Of course not," her mom agreed. "Because he'll know it's your fault."

Olivia dumped the warm rolls into a breadbasket and carried them to the table.

"It's a hard act to follow. You and Dad," she clarified, when her mother looked at her blankly.

Angela frowned. "You don't need to follow anything. You need to find your own happiness."

"If only it were that simple," Olivia lamented.

But any further discussion of the topic was derailed by her dad coming into the kitchen. Charles paused on his way to the table to take a plate of lasagna from his wife and brush his lips over hers.

It was a quick kiss—the kind that Olivia had seen them share more times than she could count. A kiss that spoke not only of shared history and easy camaraderie but also a deep and abiding love, and while it filled her with joy to see the genuine affection between her parents, it also made her heart ache just a little as she wondered if she would ever experience the same kind of connection with another person.

If Charles and Angela were to be believed—and Olivia had no reason to doubt the story of their romance—they'd only ever loved one another.

The same was true of her brother, Mitchell, who'd been in love with Lindsay Delgado since they were kids. But their happy ending had required a more circuitous route, and though Lindsay had married one of his best friends and moved to Alaska, Mitch had never fallen in love with anyone else. When Lindsay returned to Haven after the tragic death of her husband, they'd quickly found their way back to one another. First as friends, then as lovers and finally as husband and wife.

Her other brother, Michael—MG to his friends—had also fallen hard and fast. Unfortunately for MG, the love of his life had broken his heart when she left town almost twenty years earlier to pursue an acting career, and Olivia wasn't sure he'd ever managed to put the pieces back together—or if he'd even tried. Not that he was ever without a date if he wanted one, but he hadn't been in a serious relationship since Hope.

And Olivia was more than a little bit worried that her efforts to fall in love now were being thwarted by the fact that she'd given her heart away when she was fifteen and had never gotten it back again.

After school let out Friday afternoon, Olivia walked over to Diggers' for a much-needed drink and a bite to eat with Jamie Morgan.

"I didn't think this week was ever going to end," Jamie said, lifting her glass of wine to her lips.

"The week after Halloween is always a long one," Olivia agreed. "But there are only twenty-seven more school days before Christmas break."

The countdown was something they'd done since they started teaching. At first, they'd been so excited to have jobs—and grateful that they'd both secured positions at Stoney Ridge Elementary School—they'd counted down in anticipation of the first day of school. After only a few weeks, they'd started tracking the days until winter break. And then, when classes resumed after the New Year, counting down to the summer holiday.

They both loved teaching, but spending six and a half hours every day in a classroom full of kids had given them each a renewed appreciation for the time spent away from school.

"I can survive another twenty-seven days," Jamie decided. "But even more exciting than that…"

Olivia paused with her glass halfway to her lips, waiting for her friend to continue.

"…I think Thomas might be ready to propose."

"Oh, Jamie—that *is* exciting."

"He's made reservations at Cedar Point Resort on Lake Tahoe for the Veterans Day weekend and our one-year anniversary."

"I'm going to be your maid of honor, right?"

"As if I'd even consider anyone else," her friend said.

"Are you thinking a spring or fall wedding?" she asked, more than ready to discuss details, because they'd been planning their future weddings together since they were kids. And though there were pros and cons to every season, they'd agreed that summers in Nevada were too hot and winters too cold—unless it was a Christmas wedding, which Olivia had always imagined would be as magical as the season.

"I'm trying not to think at all until there's a ring on my finger," Jamie said.

"And what kind of ring?" Olivia asked. "A solitaire? A cluster? A center stone flanked by smaller diamonds?"

"You know I've always been partial to princess-cut solitaires, but honestly, I don't even care about the ring—I just want to spend my life with Thomas."

Olivia sighed wistfully. "Proof that you really are in love."

"I never thought I'd meet anyone like him—someone who suits me so perfectly, who knows everything there is to know about me and loves me, anyway."

"Thomas is pretty great," Olivia agreed.

"His friends are great, too," Jamie said. "I don't know why you won't let me set you up with one of them. Luke would be my first choice, he's—"

"I thought Thomas was your first choice," she interjected, partly to tease her friend and partly in an effort to cut off the topic of conversation.

Jamie rolled her eyes. "You know I meant my first choice *for you*. And while Nolan isn't quite as outgoing as Luke, I think he has hidden depths that you'd appreciate. And Sutter—"

"Stop," Olivia said, interrupting her friend again.

"Why am I stopping? I thought you wanted to meet someone."

"I do," she admitted. "And while being set up by our friends might make a wonderful story to tell our kids if things worked out, it's more likely that future gatherings of your friends and Thomas's friends would be awkward if they didn't."

"You're right," Jamie acknowledged. "I just want you to meet your perfect match so that you'll be as happy as I am."

It was what Olivia wanted, too. But so far, despite her best efforts, it hadn't happened for her.

"We should go shopping—to make sure you're wearing something Instagram-worthy when he gets down on one knee."

"Or I could pilfer something from your closet," Jamie said.

"Mi ropa es tu ropa."

"There's just one potential snag in my plans."

"No," Olivia said. "No snags allowed. Whatever it is, it can't possibly be as important as a romantic weekend with your soon-to-be fiancé."

"Not even helping my brother out?" Jamie said.

"Your brother's a grown man who can take care of himself," Olivia pointed out. "And isn't he going to be in Las Vegas for his ex-wife's wedding next weekend, anyway?"

Her friend nodded. "But he hinted that he'd really like me to go with him, to give him a hand with the boys."

"So he'll take your mom instead."

"Ordinarily he would," Jamie agreed. "But my aunt Mary is coming from Washington to visit next weekend."

"There has to be someone else who can help out," Olivia said. "Because there is *no way* you're cancelling your plans with Thomas."

"Well, there was one other person I thought might be willing to help..." her friend said, a hopeful note in her tone.

"Oh, no." Olivia shook her head for added emphasis.

"What if I offered to do your lunchroom duty next week?" Jamie asked.

Lunchroom monitoring was Olivia's least favorite supervisory duty and, of course, Jamie knew it.

"No," she said again, determined to hold firm.

"For the rest of the month?" her friend offered, upping the ante.

"I love you, but there's no way I'm making a road trip to Las Vegas with your brother and his three kids."

And she absolutely meant it.

Yet somehow, Olivia found herself at Morgan's Glen with a weekend bag in the back seat of her car the following Friday morning. Not because Jamie had offered an almost-irresistible bribe, but because she didn't want to risk anything getting in the way of her friend's happy ending.

And maybe because the idea of spending some real time in the company of Adam Morgan was even more enticing than freedom from lunchroom duty.

Chapter Four

Adam had just finished putting the suitcases into the back of his SUV when Olivia Gilmore's green Hyundai pulled into the driveway.

She'd dressed for the journey in faded jeans and a pink sweater with cowboy boots on her feet. Her long, dark curls tumbled freely over her shoulders, and the only hint of makeup was in the glossy sheen on her lips.

She looked casual and comfortable—his kind of woman, he thought admiringly.

Except that she wasn't.

She couldn't be.

And it would be foolish to allow himself to imagine any differently, even for a moment.

"Miss Gilmore," he said, both grateful and relieved that she'd shown up—and right on time. His sister had facilitated the arrangement with her friend, and though he'd wanted to object, he was glad not to be making the trip with the boys on his own.

"Olivia," she reminded him.

"Olivia," he acknowledged with a nod. "I appreciate your willingness to sacrifice your long weekend to take a road trip with me and the boys."

"I didn't have anything else going on," she said easily. Before he could respond to that, the back door flung open and his sons raced out of the house and down the porch steps.

"Miss Gilmore! Miss Gilmore!" Hudson was in the lead, excited to see his teacher outside of the classroom.

"Are you comin' with us?" Easton asked, his gaze on the duffel bag she'd retrieved from the back seat of her own vehicle.

Adam hadn't told his sons that they might have company on their trip, because until Olivia had pulled into the driveway, he hadn't been one-hundred-percent certain that she would show up.

"Is that okay with you guys?" she asked.

"Yes!" Hudson pumped his fist in the air.

"Yes!" Colton said, mimicking his middle brother's words and actions.

Easton, too cool to show so much enthusiasm, shrugged and said, "Sure."

"Now go get your backpacks, so we can get on the road," Adam instructed his sons, as he reached for Oliva's bag and stowed it along with the suitcases already in the back of his SUV.

They eagerly raced off again, clearly more enthused about the trip now that Olivia was joining them.

"I only booked one room at the hotel," he suddenly remembered.

"A suite, Jamie said."

"That's right," he confirmed. "Two queen-size beds in the bedroom and a pullout sofa in the living area."

"Obviously I'll take the pullout."

Which is what Jamie would have done, if she'd been the one making the trip with her brother and nephews. Still, he felt compelled to protest. "Those things aren't usually very comfortable."

Olivia shrugged. "It's only for two nights."

Two nights with this sweet, sexy woman sleeping in the same hotel suite?

The prospect made him uneasy.

Not that anything was going to happen—certainly not with three pint-size chaperones in the same suite. And yet, the mere fact that he was uneasy with the arrangement, that he was even *thinking* about the possibility that something could happen, unsettled him more than a little.

The long drive from Haven to Las Vegas was made even longer by numerous stops for bathroom breaks en route. At least they didn't have to pull off the highway every time one of the boys complained that he was hungry—which was about every five minutes—because in addition to her duffel, Olivia had brought a cooler bag packed with juice boxes and cheese strings and apple wedges and even homemade marshmallow cereal treats.

"Can I have another Rice Krispies square, Miss Gilmore?" Easton asked.

"Of course," she said, passing another treat to him.

"But since we're not at school this weekend, maybe you could all call me Olivia instead of Miss Gilmore."

"Cool," the boy responded.

At the same time, his father said, "I'm not sure that's a good idea."

"Why not?" Olivia asked.

"What if they get used to calling you Olivia and then slip up at school?"

"I've been called a lot worse," she remarked dryly. "And on purpose."

Adam wasn't convinced, but he decided to defer to her wishes, certain there would be bigger battles to fight this weekend—though hopefully not with his traveling companion.

He still had some reservations about the weekend ahead, but he was glad to have Olivia's company now. She was easy to talk to and their conversation was a pleasant distraction from the monotonous landscape.

The scent of her perfume, on the other hand, was a dangerous distraction. Because it tempted him to lean closer and inhale the seductive fragrance, to nuzzle the side of her throat and—

"You said the rehearsal is tonight?"

Olivia's question, as they passed through Tonopah, yanked his attention back to the present.

He cleared his throat. "The rehearsal's this afternoon. The rehearsal dinner is at seven tonight."

She glanced at the ETA on the map display. "You're going to be cutting it close."

"Yeah," he agreed. "Luckily, it's in one of the restaurants at the hotel."

"So you won't have to go far once we're checked in," she noted.

"You mean *we* won't have to go far," he said.

"If *we* refers to *you and the boys*, then yes," she acknowledged.

"*We* refers to *all of us*," he told her.

She shook her head. "Oh, no. I'm not going to your ex-wife's rehearsal dinner."

"Wasn't the whole point of you coming along on this trip to help me with the boys?"

"Yes," she admitted. "But there will be plenty of other people—including their mom—to keep an eye on them at dinner tonight."

"Their mom won't spend more than five minutes with them," Adam told her, keeping his voice low so that his sons wouldn't overhear him. "Her request to have them there is nothing more than a power play."

"I wonder if your request for me to go with you tonight isn't exactly the same thing."

"Maybe it is," he allowed. "Or maybe it's wanting to have someone to talk to at dinner so I don't overhear the other guests whispering about the poor ex-husband."

"No one's going to be whispering about you," Olivia said. "Or, if they are, it will be to question why the bride-to-be ever let her handsome ex-husband go."

His eyebrows lifted. "You think I'm handsome?"

"It's not what I think, it's an acknowledgement of a fact," she said, a hint of a color spreading across her cheeks before she hurried on, as if eager to shift the topic of conversation. "But it is your ex-wife's wedding weekend, and I'm a little concerned that my presence might make her uncomfortable."

"She told me that I could bring a date."

"I'm not your date," she protested.

"This weekend you are."

"I didn't sign up to be a pawn in whatever game you're playing with your ex-wife."

"That's not what this is," he denied.

She didn't look convinced. "Next you're going to tell me that she started it."

"Well, she did," he said. "By insisting that the boys— and, by extension, me—had to be at the wedding."

"You didn't want to come?"

"It's not easy for a rancher to be away from his ranch for the better part of three days."

"Are you sure that's the only reason?" she pressed.

"Of course," he said. "What else did you think it might be?"

Olivia hesitated, aware that she was pushing toward personal territory but unable to pull herself back. "Maybe you don't want to watch your ex-wife marry another man because you're still in love with her."

Adam actually laughed at the suggestion. "I can assure you that there is absolutely no possibility of that."

"Still, I think it would be best if I stayed out of sight this weekend."

"The boys will be disappointed," he said.

She was fairly certain she was being manipulated, but considering how happy his sons had been to learn that she was making the trip to Las Vegas with them, Olivia suspected it might be true—and she didn't want to be the cause of their disappointment.

"Okay," she relented. "If you really want me to go

to the rehearsal dinner tonight, I will. I just wish I was wearing something a little more suitable."

He gave her a cursory glance. Then he took another, more leisurely look, his lips curving a little as his eyes skimmed over her. His gaze, when it met hers again, was warm and appreciative, and suddenly it felt really warm inside the vehicle.

Genetics had gifted Adam Morgan with incredibly good looks and ranching had helped him build a muscular physique, and when Olivia was fifteen, he'd been so much more impressive than any of the boys she'd known from school. She'd spent a lot of time at Jamie's house while they were growing up—and her friend had spent an equal amount of time at hers—and though Adam hadn't paid them much attention, he always said "hi" with a smile, and that had been all the nurturing her crush needed to grow.

But what had tangled up her heart completely and irrevocably was the incident that occurred when she was home for the summer after her second year of college...

She was at Diggers' with some friends from high school—a group of guys and girls. They were talking and laughing, enjoying some drinks—nonalcoholic, because they were all underage—and flirting a little.

Grant Raycroft had singled Olivia out for attention, and she was admittedly flattered. The former second-string quarterback was still a good-looking guy and she felt vindicated that he'd finally noticed her, because he'd never done so in high school.

Somehow, without Olivia being quite sure how it happened, Grant managed to maneuver her outside and was attempting to talk her into taking a drive with him, so they could be alone. Olivia didn't have any trouble reading between the lines and tried to make it clear that she wasn't interested.

"Come on," he said. "You wanted me back in high school. You know you did. And now you can have me."

She could smell alcohol on his breath, though he'd only ordered Coke at the table. Maybe he'd doctored his own drinks with the same flask he'd used to spike the punch at prom. Still, she wasn't worried about being alone with him. He might have a rather high opinion of himself, but she didn't think he was dangerous.

"How do you know I wanted you in high school?"

He gave her a cocky grin. "Because all the girls did."

"Well, you were a pretty big deal back then," she acknowledged. "Now you're just a former jock coasting on the memories of your glory days in a pathetic effort to get laid."

The cocky grin turned to a sneer and his eyes went hard, forcing her to reassess the situation as he pushed her against the wall, trapping her between the brick and his body.

Then she heard Grant howl, and she opened her eyes to see that someone had grabbed his arm and twisted it up behind his back, then shoved him face-first into the brick wall.

Not someone. Adam.

"If you ever lay a hand on a woman again, Raycroft, I will break it." *His voice was low, and somehow the quiet tone made the words sound even more menacing.* "That's not a threat—it's a promise."

He let go of Grant's arm then, and the other man took a couple of steps back.

"Do you understand?" Adam asked, in the same even tone.

"Yeah." Grant glared at Olivia. "No piece of ass is worth this amount of grief, anyway."

Adam had already started to turn away, but Grant's words caused him to pivot back and swing with his fist.

Olivia gasped as the former football star fell to the ground like one of his incomplete passes.

From that moment, Adam had been more than just her best friend's hunky older brother—he'd been her hero.

Unfortunately, by that time, he'd also been married, and he was at Diggers' to pick up takeout for his expectant wife. Still, he'd given Olivia a ride home, to ensure she made it there safely...

Fast-forward to the present, and her attraction to Adam was based on so much more, because now she knew so much more about him.

She loved watching him with his boys—the attention he gave them, the way he actually listened when they talked and gave thoughtful responses to their questions. He was a great dad, involved in every aspect of his kids' lives and generous with his affection.

In addition to all that, he was still pretty hot, too.

Maybe even hotter than he'd been a decade earlier.

And maybe that was why she was suddenly feeling so warm.

"Are we there yet?" Hudson asked impatiently.

And if there had been a moment between the adults sitting up front, it was now gone.

Adam adjusted the rearview mirror to peer into the back seat, then answered his middle son's question with one of his own. "Am I still driving?"

Hudson huffed out a breath. "Yes."

"Then we're not there yet."

He shifted his attention back to Oliva then and said, in a maddeningly neutral tone, "For what it's worth, you look fine. But you can change when we get to the hotel, if you want."

The bland response made her wonder if she'd imagined the moment of connection she'd felt, fabricated the flicker of interest she saw in his eyes. Her romantic imagination running wild—again.

"Unfortunately, I didn't bring anything dressy because I was under the impression I'd be babysitting," she told him.

"Well, you look fine," he said again. "But now I have to wonder—what were you planning to wear to the wedding tomorrow?"

"I wasn't planning on attending the wedding," she said.

"But you're my date," Adam reminded her.

And though she knew it wasn't a real date, she couldn't resist the lure of even a pretend date with Adam Morgan. Though he was no longer the boy she'd secretly crushed on when she was a teenager, the man he'd grown into—a dedicated rancher and devoted father— was even more appealing to the woman she was now.

"Then I guess I'm going to be shopping in the morning."

Chapter Five

The bride-to-be and her fiancé were greeting their guests outside the restaurant entrance when Olivia and Adam arrived with the boys. Rebecca was wearing an elaborately beaded gold camisole top over a pair of cream-colored palazzo pants with high-heeled sandals. Greg was more casually dressed in tan chinos and a linen shirt with brown loafers.

Rebecca, spotting their approach, excused herself and came toward them, a practiced smile on her face.

"You're late," she said under her breath to Adam.

"Five minutes," he acknowledged.

"Late is late," she admonished, before turning to the boys without acknowledging Olivia's presence in any way. "Easton. Hudson. Colton." She crouched to enfold them in her embrace. "I'm so happy to see you."

"Congratulations on your wedding," Easton said formally.

Her laughter tinkled in the air. "The wedding's tomorrow, darling. But thank you."

"I hun-wee," Colton said.

"Dinner will be served shortly," she promised. "But first, I want you to meet your new daddy."

The boys instinctively moved closer to Adam, looking wary and uncertain about what to do next.

"Soon-to-be *step*dad," he clarified, through gritted teeth, to his ex-wife.

But he deliberately relaxed his jaw before shifting his attention to the boys.

"Go on," he urged.

While Easton and Hudson cautiously ventured forward, Colton wrapped his arms around his dad's leg.

Adam pried the little boy's arms loose and lifted him up. "This is why we're here," he reminded his son gently. "So that you can celebrate your mom's wedding with her."

"I wanna go home," Colton said, his lower lip trembling.

"You and me both," Adam muttered under his breath.

Aloud he said, "We'll go home on Sunday."

"To-mo-wo?" his youngest son asked hopefully.

"The day after tomorrow," he clarified. "Two sleeps."

Colton sighed wearily.

"But the wedding isn't until the afternoon," Olivia chimed in, hoping to give the little boy something to look forward to. "So in the morning, you can sleep in—"

Adam snorted. "I only *wish* he knew how to do that."

"—then have breakfast at the buffet," she continued, ignoring his interruption.

"Whatsa buffay?" Colton asked.

"It's a table—or lots of tables—where the food is set out on trays and platters and you get to put whatever you want on your plate and eat as much as you want."

"Like the Golden Dragon in Battle Mountain, where we sometimes go for Chinese food," Adam added to her explanation.

Colton made a face. "Egg wows fo' bwea'fist?"

Olivia held back a smile. "There probably won't be egg rolls," she said. "More likely scrambled eggs and bacon and sausage."

"An' waffows?" he asked hopefully.

"I'm sure they'll have waffles."

"I wike waffows," Colton told her.

"I do, too," she said. "And if you don't spend the whole day eating waffles, we might have time to go swimming before the wedding."

"You can't swim in the win-tuh," he said.

"You can in Las Vegas," she said. "Because the hotel has an indoor pool."

He turned wide eyes to his dad. "Can we go swimmin', Daddy?"

"Did you pack your swimsuit?"

The little boy's brow furrowed. "You packed the soo-case."

"You're right. I did." Adam scrunched up his face, much like his son had done, as he pretended to be thinking hard. "Did *I* pack your swimsuit?"

"Say *yes*, Daddy. Say *yes*," Colton urged.

Adam chuckled. "Yes, I packed your swimsuit."

"Yay!" Obviously cheered up by their discussion of waffles and swimsuits, the boy clapped his hands together, drawing the attention of his brothers, who appeared to be making awkward conversation with their mom and soon-to-be stepdad.

"But we can only go swimming tomorrow if you go over to give your mom a hug and a kiss now."

Colton wriggled to be let down, then raced over to his mom.

Adam and Olivia followed his path.

"Now you're happy to see me," Rebecca said, smiling as she accepted her youngest son's hug.

"I'm happy cuz we're gonnna go swimmin' to-mo-wo," Colton told her.

"Lucky you," she said dryly.

Adam offered his hand and his congratulations to Greg.

"Is it true?" Hudson asked hopefully. "Is there a pool here?"

"Actually, the hotel has three pools," Rebecca told them.

"And one of them has a long, twisty waterslide," Greg chimed in.

"A waterslide? Really?" Even Easton goggled at that.

While Greg continued to talk to the boys about the pool facilities, Rebecca finally shifted her gaze to acknowledge Olivia's presence.

"I'm sorry," the bride said. "I don't believe we've been introduced."

Of course, Olivia had met Rebecca before—more than once. And while she wasn't surprised that the other woman didn't remember her, she definitely remembered Rebecca. Adam's ex-wife was a stunningly beautiful blue-eyed blonde with cheekbones that could cut glass and a ridiculously narrow waist for a woman who'd given birth to three babies.

Olivia had always been on the curvy side, like her mom. And while she was generally happy with her body, standing next to Adam's ex-wife, she couldn't help but feel like one of Cinderella's much-less-attractive step-sisters.

"I'm Olivia," she said now.

But Rebecca's attention had already shifted to Adam again.

"The restaurant usually has a dress code," she said, her gaze skimming over Olivia's jeans and sweater with obvious disapproval. "But we convinced them to relax it for this event, so that the boys would be more comfortable."

"I guess that's lucky for me," Olivia said, well aware that she was the real target of the bride-to-be's barbed comment. "Because the boys had so much stuff they wanted to bring, somehow my suitcase was left on the driveway. But I'm sure you know how it is, when you travel with kids."

Adam raised an eyebrow at her obvious fib, but Rebecca's gaze narrowed, proof that Olivia's return fire had hit its mark.

Of course, the boys' mom didn't have a clue about traveling with kids, because she'd never taken them with her on any one of her numerous vacations since the divorce. At least that's what Jamie had told Olivia. And even while Rebecca and Adam were married, she hadn't taken her sons anywhere farther than the grocery store—and that was mostly just Easton, when he was a baby. Because after Hudson was born, even those treks into town were too much for her with two kids. Instead, she'd preferred to wait until Adam had finished his ranching duties for the day, so that she could leave the kids with him while she ventured out.

"Darling." Greg took Rebecca's hand. "We need to get to our table so they can start serving dinner."

"Of course," she agreed. Then to Adam she said, "You're at table number ten. You and the boys and… your guest."

Adam had no complaints about the meal, but the dinner seemed to drag on and on, and after almost nine hours on the road, he was ready to call it a night. To flop on the sofa in the hotel suite, put the hockey game on TV and crack open one of the beers he'd tucked into the cooler.

When the impromptu speeches were finally done—*thank you, God*—he was eager to make his escape. But Colton had to pee "now, Daddy!" so he took him to the men's room in the restaurant—and found himself cornered by his ex-wife again on the way out.

"I'd like a moment," she said.

Holding back a sigh, Adam sent Colton back to the table, where his brothers and Olivia were still seated, keeping his eyes on his youngest son until he'd reached his destination.

"A moment for what, Rebecca?" He gave her a pointed look. "I already apologized for the fact that we were five minutes late."

"Actually, you never did apologize," she said. "But I wanted to talk about your date."

"And her nonadherence to a nonexistent dress code?"

"No. Just the fact that you brought a date," she admitted.

"You said I could bring a plus-one," he reminded her.

"But I didn't expect that you'd bring a *date*," Rebecca protested. "I thought you'd show up with your mom or your sister."

"You made that clear," he admitted.

And her not-so-subtle dig was undoubtedly the reason he hadn't protested more vigorously when Jamie told him that her friend was going to make the trip to Las Vegas with him.

"Anyway, the boys are here—which is what you wanted," he reminded her. "So instead of wasting time trying to pick a fight with me, why don't you spend it with our children?"

"I'm not trying to pick a fight," she argued. "And the boys are getting to know their new dad."

Glancing at the table again, Adam saw that Greg was sitting in his chair, chatting with the boys and Olivia. But he refused to rise to the bait again. Because the truth was, regardless of his own feelings about their mother, he wanted Easton, Hudson and Colton to have a relationship with Rebecca, which would obviously necessitate interaction with her soon-to-be husband. And though he'd only exchanged half a dozen words with Greg, he seemed like a decent enough guy. And if he could make Rebecca happy, more power to him.

Still, Adam might have been uneasy about the boys being in the company of a man they barely knew, except that Olivia was there, too. She seemed engaged in the conversation, and he knew her presence went a long way toward making the boys feel comfortable. In fact, Colton was so comfortable with her that he'd opted for her lap rather than the chair he'd been seated in for dinner.

It was interesting, he mused, that his youngest son had taken to her so immediately and completely, because he didn't know her nearly as well as his brothers did. Easton had been in her class two years earlier and Hudson was in her class now, but it was Colton—perhaps desperate for a mother figure—who'd attached himself to Olivia as if he didn't ever want to let her go.

Another good reason why he wasn't ready to date. His boys needed all his time and attention right now. What they didn't need was to get attached to another woman who wasn't going to stick around.

Rebecca frowned as she followed his gaze. "Well, the boys certainly seem to like your new girlfriend."

No doubt Olivia would have protested the label if she'd overheard Rebecca's remark, but Adam let it slide. Not only because his personal relationships weren't any of his ex-wife's business, but also because he wasn't entirely sure how to describe his relationship with his sister's best friend.

"They do," he agreed.

"Does she spend a lot of time with them?"

"She sees them almost every day."

The dent between Rebecca's eyebrows deepened. "You must be pretty serious."

"We're here to celebrate your new relationship, not analyze mine," he said.

"I have a right to know who's spending time with my children," she said.

"And if you'd spent any time with them over the past few years, you would have heard all about Olivia."

Her gaze narrowed.

Too late, he realized his mistake.

Everything had always been a competition with Rebecca—and she always had to win. She wouldn't take kindly to the idea that another woman might be entitled to her children's affection.

"You've been seeing her that long?"

He sighed. "Olivia sees them almost every day because she's a teacher at Stoney Ridge Elementary School."

"She's your sister's friend," Rebecca suddenly realized.

"She is a friend of Jamie's," he confirmed.

"So how long have you been dating her? Or are you dating her at all?"

"Why else would she be here with me?"

Rebecca shrugged. "To help with the kids."

"She is a big help with the kids," he acknowledged.

"You're being evasive."

"Because my personal life isn't any of your business."

"We were married for four and a half years and have three children together."

"And now we're divorced, which is convenient considering that you're planning to get married again tomorrow—and to a man who calls you *Becky*, no less."

"What's wrong with that?" she challenged.

"Absolutely nothing, except that you always hated that nickname."

She shrugged. "I don't hate the way Greg says it."

There was something in her voice, an unfamiliar

softness that hinted at a sincere affection that Adam found both surprising and reassuring.

"You really do love him, don't you?"

"Why else would I be marrying him?"

"Why did we get married?" he countered.

Of course, they both knew the answer to that question—because she'd been pregnant.

They'd dated on and off in high school, and occasionally again when she came back to Haven after college, but neither of them had imagined that they'd want to spend the rest of their lives together. Not until a little plus sign appeared in the window of a home pregnancy test.

From that moment, Adam had been as committed to Rebecca as he was to the child they were going to have together. And he'd done everything in his power to make their marriage work, but the one thing he couldn't seem to do was make his wife happy.

"That's not a mistake I'd make again," Rebecca said, looking past his shoulder to the table where their sons were seated.

"Maybe we didn't plan for you to get pregnant the first time, but I don't have any regrets, and I hope you don't, either," Adam said.

"I only regret that I couldn't be the mom they deserve." Her gaze shifted again, and her lips curved a little. "But I'm hoping to change that. To spend a lot more time with them."

"They'd like that," he said, certain it was true even if he couldn't trust that Rebecca would follow through with her plan. "And I'm glad to know that you're marrying someone who seems to make you happy this time around."

"Thank you," she said graciously.

"Now I need to get our children upstairs to bed so they don't fall asleep at your wedding tomorrow," he said, eager to make his escape before his ex-wife could zero in on more holes in his *relationship* with Olivia.

Chapter Six

"Are you guys ready to head back up to the room?"

"Yes. *Please*," Easton immediately replied to his dad's question.

"It's been a long day, hasn't it?" Adam said, as he lifted Colton out of Olivia's lap and into his arms.

"A very long day," she agreed, rising from her seat.

"And *bo-or-ring*," Hudson said, deliberately drawing the word out as he and his older brother fell into step with the adults.

Olivia gasped. "What do you mean, *boring*? It was a beautiful scenic drive."

"Almost five hundred miles of desert scenery," Adam said dryly. "Not that you would have noticed, because you played video games for most of the trip."

"Because it was *bo-or-ring*," Hudson repeated.

As the two oldest boys raced the last few steps to

the elevator, Adam shifted his youngest, sleeping son to his other shoulder.

"I don't think Colton's going to get that bath you wanted him to have before bed," she noted.

"I think you're right," he agreed.

"I don't want a bath, either," Easton said.

"Me, neither," Hudson said.

"I'm not up to having this battle tonight," their dad decided.

"Does that mean we don't hafta have baths?" Hudson asked hopefully, as the elevator doors slid open.

"Not tonight," he confirmed, ushering everyone inside. "But you will need to have a bath—or shower—before the wedding tomorrow."

Hudson's finger hovered over the number panel as he tried to remember what floor their room was on.

"Ten," Adam told him.

Before Hudson could find the right button, Easton reached past him to jab it.

"Hey, it was my turn to press the buttons," Hudson protested.

"Too slow, gotta go," Easton said.

"Dad!"

He sighed. "Yes, it was your turn," he acknowledged. "So you get to use the keycard to open the room when we get there."

Olivia couldn't help but smile at the familial bickering.

"Welcome to my world," Adam said dryly.

"I'm happy to be here," she told him.

"Then you have less of a life than I do."

"That's entirely possible," she agreed, following him off the elevator.

* * *

Half an hour later, the boys were finally tucked in—Colton fast asleep in one bed with a stuffed dinosaur toy under his arm and a blanket clutched in his fist, his older brothers in the other with a blanket roll creating a wall in the middle to keep them on their respective sides. With a quiet sigh of relief that all was calm, at least for the moment, Adam ventured back to the living room, where Olivia was curled up on one corner of the sofa with an e-reader in hand.

"Will it bother you if I put the TV on?" Adam asked her.

"Not at all," she said. "I'm pretty good at tuning things out when I'm reading."

He scrolled through the channels until he found a hockey game.

"Unless it's something that I want to watch," she said, putting her tablet aside to give her attention to the game.

They watched the action in companionable silence for a few minutes, until Olivia surprised him with a quiet cheer when the Golden Knights scored a goal.

"I don't know about you, but a day with three boys tires me out more than wrangling cattle," he confided during a commercial break.

"I don't have a lot of experience wrangling cattle," she admitted with a smile. "But I do have experience wrangling kids, and they tend to have a lot of energy. But your boys are great, and that says a lot about you as a dad."

"Or my mom as a grandmother," he countered.

"Give yourself some credit," she admonished.

"I would if I thought it was something I deserved."

"As someone who spends five days a week with kids,

trust me when I say yours are great. They're not perfect," she acknowledged. "But they're respectful and kind and compassionate and helpful and—"

"Exhausting," he finished for her.

She chuckled.

"I'm going to have a beer," he decided, when the linesman whistled an offside. "Do you want one? Or do you want me to see if there's wine in the minibar?"

"Do you know what they charge for a tiny bottle of wine—or a beer—in those things?" she asked, clearly appalled by the idea of paying the ridiculously marked-up prices.

"No," he admitted.

"You could buy a regular-size bottle of wine or a six-pack of beer for the same price at the drugstore on the corner."

"Well, I happen to have a couple beers that I brought from home." He went to the cooler on the small dinette table and lifted the lid. "But I didn't think to bring any wine."

"I don't mind beer," she said. "If you're willing to share."

"I'm happy to share," he said, returning with two bottles in hand and twisting off the cap of one before offering it to her.

"Thanks." She accepted the proffered bottle. "It's cold."

"Frozen juice boxes," he said. "Much better than ice packs."

She tipped the bottle to her lips, swallowed a mouthful of beer before she ventured cautiously, "So Greg's family seemed nice."

"Yeah," he agreed.

"And they were completely charmed by the boys."

"They can be charming when they want to be."

She smiled at that. "But I don't recall seeing Rebecca's parents at all tonight."

"You wouldn't have," he acknowledged. "Because they weren't there."

"She gave you a hard time about being five minutes late and her parents didn't even make it?"

"They won't be there tomorrow, either," he said. "Apparently they're on a cruise."

"I...don't know what to say to that," Olivia admitted. "I can't imagine getting married without my parents being there."

"In fairness to Rick and Arlene, they were at the first wedding," he pointed out. "And they paid for it, too. Cutting no corners and sparing no expense so that their only daughter could have the wedding of her dreams—even if the man she was marrying wasn't one they approved of."

"You didn't get along with your in-laws?"

"We didn't *not* get along," he said. "Even when our marriage was obviously on the rocks, I tried to include them in holiday gatherings and family events, because they were Easton, Hudson and Colton's grandparents.

"But the truth is, they'd never embraced that role, and I suspected they'd been as excited about being grandparents as they were to discover—in their early forties—that they were going to be parents for the first time."

"That must have come as a surprise," Olivia murmured.

He nodded. "By their own admission, they were two

career-focused people who never planned to have children, and when Rebecca was born, they didn't know what to do with her. As a result, she was mostly left to her own devices—which undoubtedly explained how a girl like her, pampered and privileged, ended up with a boy like me.

"Still, Rick and Arlene showed up at the hospital when Easton, and later Hudson, was born," Adam continued. "They said all the right things and even opened savings accounts for each of their future educations, with additional funds added to commemorate various holidays and milestones over the years. By the time Colton came along, the Hollisters had moved to Arizona, so they didn't meet him until Christmas, when he was ten weeks old. But he got a savings account, too."

"Do they still live in Arizona?"

He nodded. "But they visit a couple of times a year, which is almost as often as Rebecca sees the boys."

"Surely you're exaggerating," Olivia said.

"Only a little."

She frowned. "Rebecca doesn't have regular visitation with her sons?"

"There's a schedule that was part of our divorce agreement, but she doesn't follow it. Instead, she pops in and out of their lives as the mood strikes. Sometimes she'll show up for a birthday, then she'll completely overlook the next. And I'm the one left trying to explain to Hudson why Mommy brought a cake for Easton but failed to call to wish him a happy day when his birthday came around. And I did try, but it's hard to make a seven-year-old understand something that even an adult can't make sense of."

She reached over to touch a hand to his arm. "And maybe you couldn't make the hurt go away, but you were there for him, and he'll always remember that."

"I hope he doesn't," Adam said. "I hope, when he grows up, he'll remember only the good stuff, not the heartaches and disappointments."

"Good stuff like road trips to Las Vegas?" she said, attempting to lighten the mood.

"Just like that," he agreed with a smile.

Cheering erupted from the television, drawing her attention back to the screen.

"Something that would make the trip even better would be if the Golden Knights scored another goal," she said.

"You really are a fan," he noted, sounding surprised.

"Two brothers," she reminded him. "And a nephew who plays."

"I should have realized that Elliott was the reason Hudson's been asking me to sign him up."

"You don't want him to play hockey?"

"My mornings are busy enough on the ranch. I can't imagine how I'd manage to get him to early hockey practices, and I already ask my mom to do too much. Plus, she's getting older and probably shouldn't be responsible for chauffeuring them around."

"It's tough being a single parent. Not that I have any direct experience," she allowed. "But I've had more than a few students who come from single-family homes—and I saw firsthand how difficult it was for Lindsay to juggle her job and two kids, even with my brother helping her out when he could."

"Mitch must not have minded too much, considering that he married her," Adam noted.

"He loves Elliott and Avenlea as much as he loves Lindsay."

"Well, I hope it works out for them."

"He says in a cynical tone," Olivia said dryly.

"If I sound cynical, it might be because I know that it takes more than love to make a marriage work."

"I don't disagree with that, but I believe that love provides a solid foundation to build on."

"How many times have you been married?"

She narrowed her gaze. "You know the answer to that."

"Right," he confirmed with a nod. "None."

"But my parents have been married for thirty-eight years," she pointed out.

"If that somehow makes you an expert on the subject, by the same logic, I should be able to fill a tooth because my cousin is a dentist."

"That's reductio ad absurdum." She lifted a hand to cover her yawn.

"I don't know what that means," he admitted. "But you're obviously tired and I should let you get to bed."

"I am to bed," she pointed out. "And I want to see who wins the game."

But when the second period ended, she did retreat to the bathroom to put on her pajamas and brush her teeth. And though Adam remained in the living room, just being in close proximity while she performed her usual getting-ready-for-bed rituals seemed to create a sense of intimacy between them.

Or maybe it was only in his imagination.

"Are you sure you don't want me to leave?" he asked when she'd returned to the living room and her spot on the sofa. "The boys are asleep now, so I can turn the game on in the bedroom."

"The TV in there is a lot smaller than this one."

"Are you saying that size matters?"

She snorted. "I have two brothers," she reminded him. "So I know that it does to men—at least when it comes to TV screens."

"That's a sexist remark."

"But is it untrue?"

"Probably not," he acknowledged.

"So how big is yours?"

He lifted his eyebrows.

Her cheeks flushed.

"Your TV at home," she clarified.

"Sixty-five inches," he admitted.

"I think you just proved my point," she said, unfolding the blanket to drape it across her lap.

She might have been focused on the game, but Adam found his gaze kept drifting away from the action on the screen to the woman beside him. Her pajamas were a waffle knit, almost like long underwear, pale pink in color with white flowers printed all over them. They weren't the least bit sexy, and yet, there was something about Olivia in them that made them look sexy, and looking at her he felt a stirring of something that he hadn't felt in a very long time. Something he didn't want to be feeling now—and definitely not for his sister's best friend.

So he forced his attention back to the TV, not realizing that Olivia had drifted off until her head tipped sideways to rest on his shoulder.

Should he wake her?

The boys always grumbled when he woke them up to tell them to go to bed.

Of course, Olivia wasn't one of the boys.

She was a woman.

A smart, beautiful, kind, generous and unexpectedly funny woman, and he was grateful not just for her help but her company.

She let out a soft sigh, and he felt the exhale of her warm breath on his throat.

Her lashes cast shadows on her cheek. Her face was scrubbed free of makeup, her skin flawless, her perfectly shaped lips parted just a little.

He was suddenly overwhelmed by the temptation to awaken her with a kiss, like Sleeping Beauty had been awakened by the kiss of her true love. Except that he wasn't a prince, and he sure as heck wasn't in love with Olivia. He was just a single dad getting a hard-on for his sister's best friend because he'd been celibate for too damn long.

And while the whole waking-someone-with-a-kiss thing might have seemed romantic in the old fairy tale, in current times, kissing a woman without her knowledge and consent was asking for a whole lot of trouble.

He should ease away from her. Settle her head on a pillow, cover her with a blanket and go to his own bed—or whatever portion of it Colton was willing to share. But he was reluctant to break the unexpected intimacy of the moment. Even if being so close to Olivia and being unable to touch her was a delicious kind of torture.

She shifted a little in her sleep, snuggling closer. Her hair tickled his chin, and he drew in a deep breath, inhaling the peachy scent of her shampoo.

He must have made some kind of sound, because she drew back abruptly, her cheeks turning pink.

"Ohmygod—I'm so sorry. I didn't mean to use you as a pillow."

"I'm used to it," he said, with a dismissive shrug.

"Still, I'd guess that having a grown woman fall asleep on you is very different than one of your kids."

"In a good way," he said, with a wink.

The pink color in her cheeks deepened, and he found himself fascinated that a fairly innocuous comment could make her blush—and wondering how she might respond if he kissed her now.

Because he really wanted to kiss her, touch her… maybe even get naked with her.

No, there was no *maybe* about it—he *definitely* wanted to get naked with her. But was he sincerely attracted to his sister's best friend? Or was his sudden awareness of her simply the result of their close proximity?

Either way, she was here and he was here, and would it really be so wrong to—

Yes! his conscience vehemently interjected. *For a whole lot of reasons—three of which are sleeping in the adjacent bedroom.*

Though he cursed his conscience for pointing out the obvious, he knew that he wasn't going to be able to look at Olivia Gilmore again and see her as anything other than a beautiful, desirable woman.

So he said good-night as soon as the game was finished, then immediately retreated to the bedroom. But he lay awake for a long time, staring at the ceiling in the dark, plagued by one inescapable fact: no matter that she was completely off-limits, he wanted her.

Per Olivia's suggestion, they had breakfast at the buffet Saturday morning. Colton was thrilled to discover that not only did they have waffles—the waffles were as big as his plate. Of course, he then went on to pile his waffle high with whipped topping and chocolate chips and sprinkles.

"It's dee-zut fo' bwea'fist," he said excitedly, as he climbed onto his chair.

"That should be enough sugar to fuel you throughout the day," Adam noted dryly.

"I needs lotsa ene-gy fo' swimmin'."

"You certainly do," Olivia agreed, sliding some berries off her own plate onto Colton's. "And fruit has the perfect amount of swimming energy."

Though Colton looked skeptical, he stabbed a raspberry with his fork.

Hudson had a waffle, too. Plus bacon and sausage. Easton filled his plate like his dad's—with eggs, sausages and hash browns.

Olivia was digging into her fruit and yogurt when her phone buzzed. Her mom had a very strict rule about no phones at the table, so she discreetly pulled it out of her pocket to peek at the screen.

It was a text message from Jamie—a picture of an engagement ring on her finger with a caption that read I said YES.

Her eyes filled with happy tears as she texted a reply offering "congratulations" followed by a string of wedding-related emojis.

"Is everything okay?" Adam asked.

She nodded and set her phone on the table so that he could see the picture on the screen.

"Someone you know got engaged," he realized.

"Someone you know, too," she told him.

"Wait—that's Jamie's hand?"

She nodded again. "Wearing a massive diamond."

A princess-cut solitaire, just like she'd wanted.

"My little sister is engaged." Though he'd initially seemed taken aback by the news, he was grinning now, obviously happy for the happy couple.

"I know who your little sister is—it's Aunt Jamie," Easton said knowledgeably.

"But what's *engaged*?" Hudson wondered.

"An engagement is a promise to marry," Olivia explained.

"Like Mom and Greg," Easton realized.

"Exactly like that," Adam agreed.

"So when are they getting married?" Hudson asked.

"That's a question you'll have to ask your aunt Jamie the next time you see her."

But for now, the boys were happy enough to turn their attention back to their plates.

"I can't believe my little sister's engaged," Adam said again, as he dumped a packet of sugar into his coffee.

"Your little sister is almost thirty," Olivia reminded him.

"You're right," he acknowledged. "Which means that

you're almost thirty, too. So why aren't you engaged? Or married?"

"Well, that's blunt," she remarked. "Shouldn't you just be grateful that I'm not engaged or married? Because if I was, I wouldn't be here to help you out this weekend."

"And I'm grateful for the help," he assured her. "But now I'm curious, too."

"My single status is hardly one of life's great mysteries—like why do we sleep? Or what was there before the big bang? And will we ever encounter intelligent alien life?"

"But it *is* a mystery," he insisted. "You're an attractive woman. Smart. Fun. Gainfully employed. And you like hockey."

"And hopefully, someday, I'll meet a guy who sees all of that *and* wants to marry me," she said lightly.

"Are you currently dating anyone?"

"Yes, but my steady boyfriend of the last six months was completely in favor of me spending a whole weekend in Las Vegas with another man—and his three kids."

"I'm sensing sarcasm."

"Look at that," she mused. "Attractive, smart and intuitive."

"I've overstepped," he noted.

She sighed. "No, you didn't. Not really."

She wrapped her hands around her coffee mug and considered how much she wanted to say sitting around a breakfast table with three children. But the boys had turned their attention back to their food and weren't paying any attention to the adults or their conversation.

"It's just a bit of a touchy subject because I do want

to get married and have a family, and I'm a little frustrated that it hasn't happened yet," she admitted. "And it's not just that I'm almost thirty. It's that everyone in my family—starting with my maternal grandparents and then my parents and each of my brothers—has fallen in love hard and fast and forever."

"And you're worried because you haven't fallen in love yet?" he guessed.

"No, I'm worried that I haven't been able to connect with any of the guys I've dated in recent years because my heart is stuck on the first boy I ever loved."

"Where is he now—the first boy you ever loved?" Adam asked curiously.

"Still way out of my league," she told him.

"How can you be so sure? I bet if you reached out to him and let him know that you were interested in trying to connect, he wouldn't turn you down."

"I'm pretty sure he would."

"Then he's a fool."

Before Olivia could respond to that, Colton held up his hands, his fingers splayed.

"I'm aw done."

"You're all sticky," Adam noted, scrubbing his son's hands with a napkin.

"That looks like a soap-and-water job," Olivia said.

"I think you're right," he agreed. "While I take him to wash up, why don't you figure out a plan for the morning with Easton and Hudson?"

"Why do we need a plan?" Hudson asked as his dad walked away.

"We wanna go swimming," Easton reminded her.

"And we will," Olivia promised. "But the pool doesn't

open until noon—more than three hours from now. So what would you like to do before then?"

"Are there go-karts?" Easton asked hopefully.

"Rock climbing?" Hudson countered.

Of course, they were in Vegas, so they could probably find any kind of entertainment that they wanted—the harder part was finding an activity that was suitable for and appealing to all ages.

"How about mini putt?" Olivia suggested, eager to make plans for the day—and grateful that Adam had walked away before she'd said too much and inadvertently revealed the truth of her feelings for him.

Chapter Seven

Adam had been to Vegas several times, and each time he couldn't help but be impressed by the spectacle that was the Strip. It was so much more than hotels and casinos, restaurants and shops, and it was a special treat to see his sons see it for the first time. The boys were dazzled by the lights, excited to point out recognizable landmarks—like the replica Eiffel Tower—delighted by the dancing water fountains at the Bellagio and thrilled to ride on a gondola through the Venetian's Grand Canal. Of course, the M&Ms store was the biggest hit with the kids—and where they spent the souvenir money that Grandma had given to them.

Through all the sightseeing, Colton clung tightly to Olivia's hand, clearly not wanting to get lost in the crowd. Of course, there really wasn't much of a crowd on a Saturday morning—certainly nothing that compared to the throng of people that would be navigating the Strip twelve hours later—but for three young boys from Haven, it was understandable that the crowd might seem overwhelming.

After all of that—and mini putt—they finally returned to the hotel to spend some time at the pool.

"The one with the waterslide," Easton had reminded them several times throughout the morning.

Olivia abandoned him then, insisting that she needed to go shopping for something suitable for the wedding but promising to meet them when she was done.

Adam was happy to discover that there were life-guards on duty at the pool. Easton and Hudson were decent swimmers, and Colton was getting there, but there was only one of him and three of them—with the youngest wearing water wings to help keep him afloat because even in the shallow end, the water was over Colton's head.

The twisty slide lived up to its promise, and Easton and Hudson were happy to climb the stairs again and again while their dad splashed around with Colton.

True to her word, Olivia joined them a short while later.

He watched as she unzipped the white hooded cov-erup she wore and whisked it over her head, dropping it on a vacant lounger, then kicked off her sandals beneath the chair and made her way to the edge of the pool.

And he tried not to stare. He really did. But he'd never suspected that beneath the stylish pants and tailored blouses she wore in the classroom was such a smokin' hot body. Even the snug-fitting denim jeans and T-shirt she'd worn earlier that morning hadn't done more than hint at the delectable curves she possessed.

And while the aqua-blue colored one-piece suit wasn't particularly revealing, it showed him curves that he'd never seen before.

She'd secured her long dark hair in a messy knot on top of her head—no doubt to keep it dry while she was in the pool—and her dark eyes were hidden beneath the lenses of her sunglasses. He wished he'd thought to bring his own, so that she wouldn't know he kept sneaking glances at her.

"You weren't gone very long," he noted, as she stepped into the water.

"I only needed one dress. And shoes."

"I've just never known a woman to get in and out of a dress shop so quickly."

"Let me guess—your ex-wife could never decide what she wanted until she'd tried on everything in the store?"

"Pretty much," he confirmed.

"And no doubt everything looked fabulous on her."

"Pretty much," he said again.

"I might enjoy shopping more if I looked like Rebecca," she confided. "Instead, I'm usually happy to find something that fits without being too clingy."

"Why the heck would you want to look like Rebecca?" he asked, sincerely confused by her remark.

"If you don't know, I'm not going to explain it," she said.

"Is it because she has the kind of figure that people think belongs on magazine covers?" he guessed.

"So you do know."

"I also know that you have the kind of curves that…"

"Curves that what?" she demanded when his words trailed off.

"That I shouldn't be noticing," he finished. "Because you're Jamie's best friend and Hudson's teacher, and I'm probably crossing a line by saying this, but your curves are spectacular."

Her cheeks colored. "I wasn't fishing for a compliment, but thank you."

"You're welcome. But please don't tell my sister I said that, because I don't need a lecture about how I shouldn't be ogling women, and especially not you."

She laughed softly. "Your secret's safe with me."

"Miz Gi-mow! Miz Gi-mow! Wook at me!" Colton launched himself off the edge of the pool and into the water, landing with a big splash that soaked Olivia.

Adam cringed, waiting for the inevitable shriek of indignation.

To his surprise, Olivia laughed.

"Who would have guessed that such a little boy could make such a big splash?" she asked.

Colton was already swimming toward the edge of the pool, no doubt to try again.

"Why don't we let Miss Gilmore enjoy the water rather than trying to drown her?" Adam suggested.

"So-wee, Miz Gi-mow," Colton said.

"There's no reason to apologize," she told him. "And I'm Olivia this weekend, remember?"

He nodded. "I 'mem-buh Miz Gi-mow."

She smiled and ruffled his wet hair.

When Easton and Hudson realized that Olivia had joined their dad and little brother in the shallow end of the pool, they abandoned the slide to join them.

Apparently the second-grade teacher was something of a celebrity in the eyes of his boys, who were obviously desperate for a woman's attention. And Olivia was wonderful with them. She listened when they talked, respected their opinions, laughed at their jokes and was firm when she needed to be.

Watching her with his boys, he found himself wondering again how it was that she wasn't married with kids of her own, because it was obvious that she was meant to be a mother.

But he'd overstepped enough for one day. Besides, her personal life was none of his business, and it was foolish to let himself wish otherwise.

Olivia had butterflies in her stomach as she fastened the narrow straps of the high-heeled sandals around her ankles. Which was silly, she knew, because this wasn't really a date.

But it felt like a date, because she was wearing a dress and makeup and planning to spend the next few hours in the company of a handsome man. Well, a handsome man and his three sons, she acknowledged to herself. But there really wasn't anyone else that she'd rather be with—and *that* was the dilemma.

She'd known it would be a mistake to make this trip with Adam and his boys, which was why she'd tried to say no when Jamie first broached the subject. But in the end, she'd been helpless to resist her friend's entreaties—and the desires of her own heart.

Secret desires that will remain secret, she promised herself as she turned to face the mirror, smoothing her hands over the skirt of her coral-colored sleeveless sheath-style dress. She was pleased with her purchase, happy to have found something that flattered her figure without seeming to flaunt it.

Would Adam like it?

It was foolish to wonder. To wish that he'd say something other than that she looked *fine*.

To hope that he'd look at her again the way he looked at her when they were at the pool earlier, when he'd told her that her curves were spectacular and sounded as if he really meant it.

But he wasn't going to say anything so long as she was hiding out in the bathroom, so she took a deep breath and opened the door.

Adam and his sons were lined up by the door, ready to go. The boys were all in khaki pants and white shirts with ties neatly knotted at their throats. Adam was wearing a dark gray suit with a lighter shirt and a black tie with gray-and-silver stripes, and her heart did a little skip and a jump inside her chest when she saw him.

The man was handsome enough in jeans and a flannel shirt. In a pair of swim trunks, all of his delicious muscles were on glorious display. But in a suit—*wow*. There were simply no other words to adequately describe how fabulous he looked dressed up.

"The Morgan boys sure do clean up nicely," Olivia remarked in a deliberately casual tone.

As if on a swivel, all four heads turned toward her.

"Finally," Easton said, as if they'd been waiting forever.

"Can we go now?" Hudson directed the question to his dad.

"You wook we-wee pwetty, Miz Gi-mow."

"Thank you, Colton." She squatted in front of him—a precarious move, considering that she was balanced on three-inch heels—to adjust the knot of the tie that he'd obviously been tugging on, and smiled when she realized there were dinosaurs cleverly hidden in the paisley design. "You look very handsome yourself."

He beamed at her.

She straightened up to inspect Hudson's tie next. His was patterned with a rodeo cowboy on the back of a bucking horse.

Moving on to Easton, she saw that what she'd initially believed to be green dots on his navy tie were actually tiny Mandalorian helmets.

"Can we go *now*?" Hudson asked again.

"As soon as Miss Gilmore finishes her inspection," Adam said, sounding amused.

"It's Olivia," she reminded him. "And I'm finished."

"You haven't checked to see that *my* tie is straight."

"I assumed that you hadn't been tugging on yours." But she played along, moving closer to check his tie, suddenly aware that the shoes she was wearing put her much closer to his eye level. And when she lifted her gaze, she found his locked on her. "Your tie is…fine."

She nearly winced when the word came out of her mouth.

The corners of Adam's eyes crinkled as his lips curved. "Now it's my turn."

She swallowed. "Your turn?"

His gaze warmed as it moved over her, from the twist of hair that she'd secured on top of her head all the way down to her sandals, lingering at strategic points in between.

"Wow."

The single word, softly spoken, made her heart pound and her knees weak.

"We're gonna be late," Hudson grumbled, shattering the intimacy of the moment.

"We're *not* going to be late." Then Adam looked at Olivia again, his tone regretful when he said, "But we do need to be going."

She nodded.

"I get to do the elevator this time," Easton said, already reaching for the handle of the door.

"I get to do it when we come back," Hudson countered, right behind his brother.

"I wanna do it, too," Colton piped up.

"Are you ready for this?" Olivia asked Adam, as they followed the boys out the door.

"I'm ready." He took her hand, twining their fingers together. "And I'm really glad you're here."

"I'm glad I let you talk me into being your date tonight," Olivia said, as they lingered at the table long after dessert and coffee had been served. "That meal was fabulous."

"And here I thought it was my company and conversation that you were enjoying," he said dryly.

She smiled. "That, too."

There was something about her smile, something both sweet and sexy that made him wonder what kind of lover she would be. Sweet? Or sexy? Or, like her smile, a combination of both?

Not that he was ever going to find out, but it was kind of fun to wonder.

Completely inappropriate, but fun.

Aware that he was staring, he deliberately shifted his gaze to look over her shoulder to the table where Greg's parents were seated. Easton, Hudson and Colton had been invited to join them there, and though hesitant at first, learning that Roger Burnett had spent a lot of years working on a stock-car pit crew had piqued enough interest to overcome their reluctance. Because they'd been fascinated by race cars since Santa made the mistake of putting Hot Wheels in their stockings one Christmas.

But Adam didn't really mind. He knew it was important for the boys to learn that there was more to life than cattle and horses. And he was genuinely pleased that the boys had a new step-grandfather who seemed to take an interest in them. His own dad had been gone for almost five years now, and while Easton had some memories of Grandpa Mike, Hudson's were hazy at best and Colton, who'd been only a few months old when his grandfather passed, had none.

Shaking off the melancholy, he picked up the bottle of wine on the table to refill Olivia's glass.

"You're going to have three kids and an inebriated schoolteacher to look after if I drink any more wine," she warned.

"You mean drunk?" he asked, sounding amused.

She shook her head. "Teachers don't get drunk."

"Then you have nothing to worry about."

Truthfully, Olivia wasn't worried about the wine so much as the man. Because being with Adam—even on a pretend date—was far more intoxicating than even the top-shelf liquor being poured at the bar. Just sitting close to him was enough to make her knees weak.

She was supposed to be doing a favor for Jamie. She wasn't supposed to be falling back into old habits, crushing on her best friend's big brother.

"Do you want to dance?"

Adam's question jolted her out of her reverie. "Oh… Um…"

"It's a simple yes-or-no question," he said, sounding amused.

Olivia suspected there wasn't anything simple about it, that if she let herself dance with him—something she'd only dreamed about doing—she might start to wish that all her other dreams starring Adam Morgan might come true, too.

"The boys—"

"Are with their new step-grandparents," he interjected.

"How do you feel about that?"

"You're supposed to be my date, not my shrink."

"Except that we both know I'm neither of those things."

"Let's see if you can at least pretend to be my date—or pretend to know how to dance."

Her gaze narrowed. "I know how to dance."

"Prove it."

She accepted his proffered hand, unable to resist his challenge. Or maybe unable to resist the opportunity to finally be held close by the boy she'd been infatuated with for more years than she wanted to admit.

She lifted her hand to his shoulder, where she could feel his muscles flex beneath her palm. He put his other hand at her waist, and the heat of his touch seemed to brand her skin.

She didn't recognize the song, so she concentrated on following his lead. She stumbled a little when he drew her closer—close enough that her breasts were almost touching his chest—and wondered if he could hear her heart beating.

"I have a confession to make."

The words, whispered close to her ear, made her shiver. "What's that?"

"I like the way you feel in my arms."

"Maybe you're the one who's had too much to drink," she said lightly.

"And you smell good," he said, ignoring her response. "Not at all like bubblegum or baby shampoo."

She managed a laugh, pretending that his nearness wasn't wreaking havoc on her hormones.

But there was another moment, as the song was drawing to a close, when she tipped her head back and found him looking at her. When his gaze dropped to her mouth, and lingered there for a long moment.

Her breath caught in her throat as she realized that he was thinking about kissing her. Or maybe she was projecting, because she desperately wanted him to kiss her. Desperately wanted to know if the fantasy that had lived in her heart since she was fifteen could possibly translate to reality.

And just when she thought he would breach the scant distance that separated their mouths, he instead took a hasty step back.

"It's getting late," he said.

She nodded. "We should get the boys upstairs and into bed before they conk out."

"Not that they seem to be in any danger of that anytime soon," he noted.

Following his gaze, she spotted the boys—apparently coaxed onto the dance floor by their new grandparents—wiggling and shaking to the Black Eyed Peas.

"No doubt they're on a sugar high from all the icing on the cake, but the crash will come soon enough."

With an apology to Greg's parents for breaking up the dance party, Adam herded the boys away, reminding them that it was past their bedtimes.

"But I not ti-wood," Colton protested.

"Well, we're going to find your mom to say goodnight and you can be not tired upstairs," Adam told him.

It didn't take them long to track down the newlyweds. Of course, the bride was pretty easy to spot, being as she was the one in the fancy white dress.

"Congratulations on your wedding," Easton said again.

"We're so glad you could celebrate with us," his new stepdad said, shaking hands with each of the boys and then Adam and Olivia, too.

Rebecca gave her sons big kisses, leaving smears of pink lipstick on their cheeks.

"Thank you," she said to Adam. "For bringing the boys for the wedding."

"I was happy to."

An appropriate response, Olivia mused, if not an entirely truthful one.

"I want you to know that I plan to spend a lot more time with them in the future," Rebecca told him.

"We can look at revising the visitation schedule whenever you want," he said agreeably.

"I'm not talking about visitation."

Adam's expression grew wary. "Then what are you talking about?"

"Becky? Honey?" Greg touched a hand to her arm. "The limo's waiting for us outside."

"Okay." Then, to her ex-husband, she said, "I have to go. But I'll call you, and we'll pick up this conversation when I'm back from my honeymoon."

"What conversation?" he wanted to know, but the bride and groom had already walked away.

"Whatsa honeymoon?" Colton asked.

Adam was frowning, obviously still thinking about Rebecca's parting words, so Olivia answered the little boy's question.

"A honeymoon is a vacation that a bride and groom take after their wedding," she told him. "Your mom and stepdad are going to Aruba—an island in the Caribbean. I'll show it to you on a map when we get back to the room."

"I get to press the buttons this time," Hudson said, racing toward the bank of elevators.

"I wanna do da buttons," Colton whined.

"Will you *stop* with the *damned buttons*?" Adam snapped.

His youngest son's lower lip trembled, his eyes filling with tears as he clutched at Olivia's hand. "Why's Daddy mad?"

"I think your mom's been pushing his buttons."

The little boy shook his head. "Daddy does'n have buttons."

Olivia didn't argue. It was obvious from the stricken

expression on Adam's face that he felt bad enough for lashing out at his child.

He crouched down in front of Colton now. "I'm sorry, buddy. It's been a really long day and Daddy's a little cranky because he's tired."

"Dad—the elevator's here," Easton called out.

"I'll go up with Easton and Hudson," Olivia said. "Why don't you and Colton take the next one so that he can push the buttons?"

Adam sent her a grateful look. "Thanks."

She glanced at Colton then. "Is that okay?"

He nodded and slowly released the vise grip on her hand to reach for his dad's.

Chapter Eight

Despite Colton's protests that he wasn't tired, the little boy's eyes drifted shut long before story time was over. Olivia finished reading the book he'd requested, anyway, then closed the cover and set it on the table beside the bed.

"You know he zonked out before Harold even drew the hungry moose and deserving porcupine to eat all the leftover pies, don't you?" Adam said from the doorway.

"I do," she confirmed. "But *I* wanted to know how the story ended."

He chuckled. "You haven't read that book to your class a hundred times?"

"Considering that I've only been teaching seven years, I can confidently say that I have not."

"Thirty minutes," he said, speaking to Easton and Hudson now.

They both nodded, already engrossed in their own books, and Adam guided Olivia to the living area, leaving the bedroom door ajar.

"Are you feeling less cranky now?" she asked him.

"Yeah." He scrubbed his hands over his face. "Sorry about that."

"You don't have to apologize to me—and you already apologized to Colton. I only mentioned it in case it was something you wanted to talk about."

"I might want to talk if I knew what the *something* was," he said. "But Rebecca has a habit of making cryptic remarks that I don't know how to interpret."

"Pushing your buttons," she said again.

"Yeah." He sighed. "I can only hope that she'll turn her attention to pushing Greg's buttons now that they're married."

"That's a happy thought." Olivia sank onto the sofa, grateful to kick off the shoes she'd bought because the salesperson had convinced her they were perfect for the dress.

She hadn't been wrong, but Olivia wasn't accustomed to wearing such high heels, and as she started to tuck her legs beneath her, she sucked in a sharp breath as her left foot cramped.

"You okay?" Adam asked.

She jumped up and started to hobble around, trying to flex her foot to relieve the pain.

"Foot cramp," she said through gritted teeth.

He sat on one end of the sofa and clapped his hands against his thighs. "Give it to me."

"What?"

"Your foot," he clarified. "Let me massage out the cramp."

"I'm not letting you massage my feet."

"You'd rather hobble around in pain?"

She huffed out a breath and plopped back on the sofa, lifting her legs so that her feet were in his lap.

He picked up her left foot and began to work the sole with his thumbs.

She sighed with pleasure and let her head fall back. "Oh. Wow. You're really good at that."

"You're not the first woman to say so," he told her. "But it's not usually in response to a foot rub."

"Ha ha," she said, though she was sure he wasn't entirely joking.

When he'd finished working his magic on the left foot, he moved on to the right.

"I wasn't sure how this was going to work when Jamie told me that she'd enlisted you to accompany us this weekend," he said. "But I'm really glad you were here."

"I had a good time," she said, and meant it.

"I mostly did, too—and believe me, that was a surprise."

"It didn't bother you to watch your ex-wife exchange vows with another man?"

He shook his head. "Rebecca and I were over a long time ago. I'm happy she's moved on."

"How about you?" she asked, eyeing him closely. "Have *you* moved on?"

"I want to," he said. "But as a rancher and a single dad, I don't really have time for a romantic relationship, though there are moments, like tonight, when we were dancing, that I wish I did."

"Are you saying that…you're attracted to me?"

"It seems so."

"I did *not* see that coming," she admitted.

She'd hoped, of course. For a lot of years, she'd hoped that he would someday look at her as a woman and want her as she wanted him. But she'd begun to despair that it would ever happen.

"Neither did I," he admitted.

"You're the one who asked me to dance," she reminded him.

"You're right," he acknowledged. "And I don't regret it. What I regret is that holding you made me want more—but I'm not in a position to offer you anything more."

"Have I asked you for anything?"

"No. But if I had to guess, I'd guess that you're not the type of woman who'd be happy with a friends-with-benefits arrangement."

"And you'd be right," she said. "But I can be your friend-without-benefits."

"Then I guess that will have to do."

"How was your trip?" Gramma Shirley asked, when the weary travelers made their way into the house.

Her grandsons immediately surrounded her, offering hugs and kisses and chattering excitedly.

They'd only been gone for two days, but it was obvious to Adam that the boys had missed her. Not that he was surprised. Since she'd moved in with them more than four years earlier, they hadn't ever been away from her for two full days.

While they told her about mini putt and swimming and

the big fancy cake at the wedding—understandable priorities for five-, seven- and nine-year-olds—he took advantage of the opportunity to catch up with his mother's sister.

"I didn't think we were going to get to see you," Adam said, giving his aunt Mary a big hug.

"I was originally planning to head back to Washington this morning, but it seemed a shame to come all this way and not see my favorite nephew and great-nephews."

"I'm your only nephew," Adam reminded her.

"You'd be my favorite, anyway," she assured him.

"You want a cup of tea?" he asked, as his mom ushered the boys upstairs to get ready for bed.

"I'd rather have a beer, if you've got one."

"Me, too," he said, taking two bottles from the fridge and twisting off the caps.

"I imagine it was a long drive with three usually active boys strapped into the back seat," Mary noted.

"It definitely was," he confirmed.

"But I hear you had some adult company, too."

"Yeah." He lifted the bottle to his lips, took a long swallow. Not because he didn't want to tell his aunt about Olivia, but because he honestly wasn't sure what to say. He'd been spared having to make introductions as Olivia had been eager to get home to her own house, moving from the passenger side of his SUV to the driver's seat of her own vehicle, pausing only long enough to grab her bag and give quick hugs to the boys.

"Shirley didn't mention that you were seeing anyone."

"I'm not."

"So the woman who spent the weekend in Las Vegas with you and your sons is…your nanny?"

He snorted. "As if I could afford a nanny."

"So…who is she?"

"Her name is Olivia."

"Jamie's friend?" she guessed.

He nodded.

Her gaze took on a speculative gleam.

"So how was your weekend?" he asked, eager to divert a potential interrogation.

"It was wonderful," she said. "Your mom and I went into town, we did some shopping, had lunch, treated ourselves to mani-pedis."

"I'm glad," he said. "Mom's always so busy taking care of everyone else, she sometimes forgets to take care of herself."

"We stopped by the feed store, too, to pick up the poultry fencing that you'd ordered."

He frowned. *Poultry fencing?* "You mean chicken wire?"

"Yeah, but your mom called it poultry fencing."

He swallowed a mouthful of beer.

"Forgetting common words can be a symptom—"

"Maybe she didn't forget the words," he interjected. "Maybe she just thought poultry fencing was a better description."

"Have you noticed any changes in her behavior recently?" Mary asked gently.

"No." He lifted the bottle to his lips again. Sighed. "Actually, something did happen…several weeks back. It's probably nothing." He *hoped* it was nothing. "But one night, late in September, Mom woke up in the middle of the night and wandered outside. Thankfully, I'd put a bell on the exterior doors when the boys were little, so that I'd know if they tried to get out of the house, and I heard it when the door opened.

"I found her at the end of the driveway, peeking into the mailbox at four a.m. When I asked her what she expected to be delivered at that hour of the morning... she giggled and said she was expecting a letter from Michael Morgan."

"Your dad frequently wrote letters to her when they were dating," Mary noted.

Adam nodded. "I know. She kept them all. They're in a box in her bedroom closet."

"Shirley was prone to sleepwalking when she was a child."

"So that's probably what she was doing—sleepwalking and talking to me in her dream. Which is why she didn't have any memory of the event when I asked her about it the next day."

"That's one explanation," his aunt agreed.

"What else could it be?" he asked, and immediately wished he could take back the question.

She met his gaze evenly. "Early onset dementia."

"No." He refused to consider the possibility.

"Your grandmother had Alzheimer's," Mary reminded him.

"I know. But she was in her late seventies before she started exhibiting any symptoms. Mom is still two years away from her sixtieth birthday."

"That would be the early onset part," his aunt said gently.

"No," he said again.

It was too soon for his mom to be experiencing any kind of cognitive decline.

He needed to believe it was too soon.

He needed it to *be* true.

Because she wasn't just his mother, she was his anchor. And his kids' anchor, too.

And, thinking back to Rebecca's cryptic remark, he wasn't sure he could handle the storms to come without her.

"How was your weekend in Las Vegas?" Angela asked, when Olivia showed up for dinner Wednesday night.

She responded with a single word: "Exhausting."

Her mom chuckled. "I had three kids myself. I know how busy they can be."

"The Morgan boys are definitely that."

"I'm sure Adam was grateful for your help."

"I think so."

"And how was Jamie's weekend?"

Olivia grinned. "I'd say it positively sparkled."

"Thomas proposed?"

She nodded and pulled her phone out of her pocket to show her mom the picture that Jamie had sent. "She's already asked me to be her maid of honor."

"As if there was ever any doubt," Angela said. "You two have been thick as thieves since grade school."

And Olivia *was* sincerely happy for her friend—but maybe just the teensiest bit envious, too.

"So what else is going on with *you*?" her mom asked now. "Any news to share about that doctor you've been dating?"

"I'm not sure that two dates in three months can be called dating." Olivia tossed the green salad she'd made with her mom's homemade balsamic dressing. Unlike at Olivia's house, there were no store-bought salad dressings in Angela Gilmore's refrigerator.

"What happened? I thought you two had really hit it off."

"I thought so, too. But it's hard to make plans with someone who's always on call at the hospital." She licked a splash of dressing off her thumb. "Actually, that's not true. It's easy to make plans, but not so easy to keep them."

"You knew that he was an ER doctor when you agreed to go out with him," her mother reminded her.

And his career had undoubtedly been part of the appeal. But that was before she'd discovered that he was dedicated to his work to the exclusion of all else. And while she appreciated that anyone doing the same job would need to be, she wanted someone to share her life—not just a few hours every couple of weeks.

And, yes, she was well aware of how selfish that sounded. After all, the man had never canceled plans with her to hang out with his buddies or watch a big game on TV—he was literally saving lives! And she was sincerely grateful that he was able to do so, but the reality of dating a doctor was a lot less exciting than the idea.

"We still text occasionally and, every once in a while, try to make plans to get together, but so far our schedules haven't meshed."

"Maybe that's a sign," Angela acknowledged. "Because as appealing as it might seem to be married to a doctor, you want a husband who will be there when your children are born."

"Whoa!" Olivia held up a hand. "Don't you think you're jumping the gun a little, talking about marriage and children? We've only had two dates."

"But isn't that why you're dating him? To determine if he's the kind of man you want to spend your life and have a family with?"

"I guess it is," she acknowledged. "I just don't believe in making wedding plans until after at least the third date."

"As if you haven't had every detail of your wedding planned since you were twelve years old," Angela said.

"I like to think my tastes are a little more sophisticated now than when I was twelve. Although I'd still go for the chocolate fountain for dessert."

Her mom chuckled.

"There's a chocolate fountain for dessert?" Charles asked, coming into the kitchen.

"Sorry," his wife said. "But there are chocolate cupcakes."

"Even better," he said. "But why were you talking about chocolate fountains?"

"Because Olivia wants one at her wedding."

He frowned at his daughter. "You're getting married?"

"I hope so. Someday."

"Oh." He exhaled a sigh of relief. "Someday is good. You don't need to rush into anything."

"She's almost thirty," Olivia's mom pointed out unnecessarily.

"Thirty is young," her dad said.

"I was twenty-four when we got married," Angela reminded him. "You were twenty-five."

"Too young to get married," he insisted, drawing his wife into his arms. "And too much in love to do anything else."

Angela smiled, obviously just as much in love with her husband now as she'd been thirty-eight years earlier.

It warmed Olivia's heart to see her parents like this. They were tangible proof to her that when you found the right person, love could and did endure. Of course, their lives hadn't been without trials and tribulations, but their commitment to one another had helped them not just pull through but come out even stronger on the other side.

"Now that's enough of that nonsense," Angela said, pulling away from her husband after a lingering kiss. "I've got food to put on the table."

"Nonsense?" Charles shook his head. "What kind of woman considers romance to be nonsense?"

"One who's been married to you for almost forty years and knows how grumpy you get if dinner isn't on the table at six o'clock."

"She's right," he confided to their daughter. "Ranching is hard and I work up an appetite."

"Even though you do more supervising than ranching these days," Angela pointed out.

"Right again," he acknowledged. "Now that I've got two sons who are capable of doing the heavy lifting."

"I can do anything my brothers can do," Olivia reminded him.

"I know it," Charles assured her. "With the added benefit of looking just as pretty as your mom doing it."

"While I appreciate the compliment," she said, "I'd rather be recognized as a smart woman than a decorative one."

"You are smart," her dad agreed. "Hopefully too smart to marry a rancher."

"Why don't you want me to marry a rancher?" she asked curiously.

"Because he'll be out of the house from sunup to sundown and constantly grumbling about land taxes or the market price of beef."

"Or both," Angela said.

"Or both," he confirmed.

"And yet, between the chores and the grumbling, you managed to be there for the births of each of our children," Angela reminded him.

"Of course I was," he said. "Though I barely made it in time for Olivia's."

"Only time in your life you were ever early," Angela said to her daughter, softening the words with a smile.

"I went from helping Sundance deliver a breach foal to racing into the house to catch your arrival into the world," Charles said. "Literally."

"I hope you at least washed your hands in between," Olivia said dryly.

"I don't honestly remember if I did." Her dad grinned. "Either way, you don't seem any the worse for wear."

Thankfully, conversation moved on to other topics while they ate their dinner, with no mention of land taxes or beef prices, either.

She enjoyed these weekly meals with her parents, but her attention drifted a little as her mom started talking about the upcoming church bazaar, and she found herself recalling some of the conversations she'd had with Adam and his boys while they were in Vegas. It was true that kids said the darnedest things, and there had never been a dull moment at the table.

Someday I'll have a family of my own, Olivia promised herself.

She reluctantly passed on dessert, having stuffed herself on dinner. But she did linger over a cappuccino while her parents enjoyed dessert—her dad devouring three of the cupcakes his wife had made with cherry filling and chocolate ganache frosting.

After dishes were done, Olivia kissed each of her parents goodbye and headed back to town with a container of leftover meat loaf and mashed potatoes.

She'd just pulled into her driveway when her phone chimed to indicate a text message.

It was from Leo Delissio—the doctor her mom had been asking her about earlier (aka, Dr. Delicious, as Jamie had nicknamed him because he was so yummy-looking).

I'm not on call Sat night. Want to try dinner again?

The first few times he'd reached out, she'd felt a little frisson of excitement that the handsome doctor was showing an interest in her. But she'd been disappointed too many times to let herself get her hopes up.

Still, she didn't hesitate to reply:

Yes :)

Because despite her mother's warning and her own reservations, she wanted to fall in love, get married and have a family. And though she hadn't spent a lot of time with the doctor, she thought he'd make a good husband and father. More important, he was the only man she'd dated in a long time who'd shown any interest in a real relationship.

Unbidden, an image of Adam Morgan filled her mind. For that one brief moment, sitting on the hotel sofa with her feet in his lap, she'd been certain that he was going to kiss her, and she'd felt not just a frisson, but exploding rockets of excited anticipation.

But the kiss had never happened.

Instead, the moment had passed almost before it had begun.

She shook off the memory and the regret as another message popped up on the screen.

Great. I'll make a reservation at The Home Station for 7.

Or I could make dinner for you here.

I think I owe you a meal. Or two or three.

She appreciated his acknowledgment of their canceled plans but was still a little wary about being stood up—or abandoned—again.

If we're at my place, I won't be stuck eating alone in public if you have to run out.

Ouch.

I'm sorry. I wasn't trying to be hurtful, just honest.

No need to apologize for speaking the truth. And actually, your place sounds great, but I'll bring dinner from THS.

That sounds even better.

She carried her leftovers into the house, feeling cautiously optimistic about her prospects of eating something other than her mom's meat loaf Saturday night.

Chapter Nine

Olivia was in the staff room Thursday morning, pouring a mug of coffee, when Jamie came in and made a beeline for the coffeepot.

She handed the mug to her friend. "You look like you need it more than I do."

"Thanks," Jamie said gratefully, adding a splash of milk and two heaping spoonfuls of sugar to the coffee.

Olivia reached into the cupboard for a second mug. "Were you and your fiancé up late making wedding plans?"

It had, understandably, been her friend's favorite topic of conversation since Thomas had put the ring on her finger.

Jamie shook her head. "I didn't even see Thomas last night."

"I thought you were going to look at potential venues." Olivia added milk and half a teaspoon of sugar to her own mug.

"That was the plan," Jamie agreed. "Until Adam called me after school yesterday and asked me to drop by."

At the mention of her friend's brother, Olivia's heart skipped a beat, as it had been doing for almost half of her life. But she ignored it, as she'd also been doing for almost half of her life.

Of course, she'd had a little more trouble forgetting about him since their trip to Vegas and the almost kiss. But she'd done her best to put him out of her mind, because he'd made it clear that he wasn't interested in a relationship and Olivia wanted more than the friends-with-benefits arrangement he'd seemed amenable to.

Which was why she was having dinner with Leo rather than Adam on Saturday night. Well, that and the fact that Adam hadn't asked her. In fact, she hadn't heard a single word from him since their return from Vegas.

"What's the problem?" she asked Jamie now, trying to sound casual.

Her friend glanced at the clock. "It's a long story, and the first bell's going to ring soon. Can we talk at lunch?"

Olivia shook her head regretfully. "I'm covering Kevin's supervision duty at lunch."

"And I've got after-school duty," Jamie said.

"Dinner at Diggers'?" she suggested, her curiosity really piqued now.

"How about pizza from Jo's? I'll pick it up and bring it to your place."

Which meant that Jamie wanted to talk but also

wanted to be sure that no one else would be able to overhear what they were talking about.

"That works," Olivia agreed.

Jamie managed a smile, though it was obviously strained. "Thank you."

Olivia gave her a quick hug. "Remember—there's only nineteen more school days until the winter break."

Olivia had plates and napkins on the coffee table, an assortment of crudités arranged around a bowl of ranch dip and bottle of pinot noir opened beside two glasses when her friend arrived with the pizza.

"Someone's been talking to her class about well-balanced meals," Jamie teased.

"It's part of the curriculum," Olivia reminded her as she poured the wine. "But also—I was hungry, so I nibbled on some veggies while I was waiting."

Jamie lifted her glass and gulped some wine.

"That bad?" Olivia asked, opening the lid of the pizza box.

"It might be even worse," Jamie said, transferring a slice to her plate, then adding a handful of veggies and a spoonful of dip. "Or it might be nothing at all."

Olivia settled on the sofa with her food and her wine.

"Tell me," she urged.

Jamie swallowed another mouthful of wine. "Rebecca's not even back from her honeymoon and she's creating havoc for Adam."

"How?"

"By suing for custody of my nephews."

Olivia's stomach churned. "She wants *custody*?"

"Adam was served by her new lawyer yesterday."

"I'm not sure I want to imagine how he responded to that."

"There were a lot of four-letter words," Jamie confided.

"Those boys are his world." If she'd had any doubts about it before, they'd been put to rest over the weekend she'd spent with them in Vegas.

Her friend nodded.

"I don't understand why she suddenly wants custody of the sons she doesn't even see on any kind of regular schedule," Olivia admitted. "Or why she thinks a judge would give it to her."

"She's claiming that her marriage is a material change in circumstances and that she's now in a better position than Adam to provide the boys with a stable home environment."

"There's no way she'll win…is there?"

"I hope not," her friend said, though Olivia could hear the worry in her tone. "But I've been doing some reading, and it does seem that courts show a preference for placing kids in a two-parent family when that's an option."

"I hope you didn't share that with your brother."

"Of course I did," Jamie said. "I also told him how he can level the playing field."

"I'm not sure I want to know."

"He needs to get married."

Rebecca's application for custody had been locked in the bottom drawer of Adam's desk since he'd been served with the papers. He'd wanted them out of sight so that the boys couldn't stumble upon them. Unfortunately, out of sight did not mean out of mind, and he'd hardly been able to think about anything else since he'd read them.

But he made an effort for his sons, pretending everything was normal when they sat down together for dinner Thursday night.

"How was school?" he asked.

"Fine," Hudson responded.

"Great," Colton chimed in, then proceeded to tell him, in excruciating detail, absolutely everything that had happened in his kindergarten class from the first bell in the morning until the last bell in the afternoon.

"How was your day, Easton?" Adam prompted, when they'd started to clear the table after eating and he realized his oldest son had remained mostly silent throughout the meal.

Easton responded with a shrug.

"Do you have any homework tonight?"

"Just a page of math problems."

"You go on and do that," Shirley said. "I'll finish up here."

"Thanks, Gramma."

"I've got homework, too," Hudson said.

"Then you're excused, too," she told him.

"Yay!"

Adam sighed. "I'm trying to teach them responsibility."

"Doing homework is responsible," she said.

He could hardly disagree with that, so he turned to Colton instead and asked, "Did you get a new book at the library?"

"I gots fwee," Colton said, displaying three fingers.

"Well, why don't you go pick the one—" he held up one finger "—that you want us to read tonight before bed while Gramma and I finish tidying up."

Colton was just as ecstatic as his brothers to be excused from his usual chores and hurried off to fulfill his dad's request.

"Did Easton seem a little moody tonight?" he asked his mom, as they worked side by side in the kitchen.

"He was quieter than usual," Shirley noted.

"I'll try to talk to him before bed, but I suspect he's just being a tween."

"Are you going to tell the boys about Rebecca's application?"

He sighed. "Not until I have to. And definitely not before I've seen my own lawyer."

"Have you made an appointment?"

"I called Katelyn Gilmore's office today. The earliest she could get me in is late Saturday afternoon."

Which meant that he had another forty-six hours to wonder and worry before he got to talk to his lawyer, who happened to be Olivia's cousin.

"I can understand why you're concerned," Shirley said gently. "But no judge is going to send your boys to live with a mother who's seen them twice in the past six weeks."

"Three times, if you count the wedding," he noted.

"This is their home. This has always been their home and it will always be their home."

He nodded, wishing he could feel reassured.

But he knew the only reason he'd been able to manage the ranch and take care of his sons was because his mom had been there to help. And the recent episodes…

if they were a sign of dementia… Well, that kind of diagnosis would be horrible for so many reasons, but right now, selfishly, the biggest reason was that a judge might decide she wasn't capable of helping him care for his children.

No point in borrowing trouble, he reminded himself.

As of now, there had been only two minor episodes at home. (And one at the grocery store that he wouldn't even call an episode, because anyone could forget a wallet.) So maybe he needed to do a little bit more around the house to help his mom help with the boys—because nothing was more important to him than keeping his family together.

After his mom had settled in the living room with a cup of tea and *Wheel of Fortune*, Adam tucked Colton and Hudson into their respective beds, then knocked on Easton's door before stepping into his room.

"Did you finish your math?"

"Yeah," Easton answered without glancing up from the graphic novel in his hand.

"Did you want me to check it over?"

"No."

Adam wasn't offended by the response. His oldest son might have struggled with his reading when he was younger, but he was a wiz when it came to numbers.

He lowered himself onto the edge of the mattress. "Do you want to tell me what's going on with you?"

"No," Easton said again.

He bit back a sigh. "Let me rephrase—please *tell me* what's going on with you."

"Nothin'."

"It doesn't seem like *nothin'*," Adam said. "It seems like a pretty big *somethin'* because you've barely said a dozen words since you got home."

"Why should I tell you anything when you don't tell me anything?"

"I'm going to need you to explain that."

Easton finally closed his book, looking at Adam with eyes filled with anger and frustration…and maybe a little bit of fear.

"I overheard you and Aunt Jamie last night," he admitted.

"You mean you eavesdropped on me and Aunt Jamie," Adam said.

"I got up to get a glass of water—I didn't even know she was here until I heard you talking."

"What, specifically, did you hear?" he asked, though he was pretty sure he knew the answer to the question—and the reason his eldest son was obviously out of sorts.

"I heard you tell her that Mom could get custody of us."

Adam scrubbed his hands over his face and silently cursed himself for having a conversation with his sister where his boys could overhear. Of course, he'd assumed they were asleep and, therefore, hadn't held back from sharing his deepest, darkest worries with Jamie.

"Is it true?" Easton asked him now. "Will we have to go live with Mom?"

"The only thing that's one-hundred-percent certain right now is that your mom has talked to a lawyer about changing our current custody agreement."

"But why? We hardly ever even see her—why would she suddenly want us to live with her?"

"I don't know what her reasons are," Adam admitted. "And I don't want you to worry about what you over-heard. I was simply expressing concerns to Aunt Jamie, but I don't really believe she can win custody."

"You don't?"

"No, I don't," he said firmly. "I'm not going to prom-ise that it couldn't happen, but I'm hoping that your mom and I can come to some kind of agreement where she gets to spend more time with you and your brothers, but you'll continue to live here with me."

"What if *you* got married?" Easton said.

"Where did *that* come from?"

"Aunt Jamie said that Mom has a better chance of get-ting custody because she's married now—because the judge might think that two parents are better than one."

"I don't think that's true," Adam said.

"But what if a judge thinks it is?" his son pressed.

"We'll worry about that if and when it happens."

"But if you were married—"

"It's not that simple, Easton," he said, silently cursing his sister for expressing such a ridiculous idea out loud.

"Why can't it be?"

"I can't just go out and ask someone to marry me."

"I know," Easton said, nodding. "You need to take her out on a date and kiss her, and then you ask her to marry you."

"And I haven't been on a date since…actually, since your mom and I were dating."

"So go on a date now. Gramma's here to watch me and Hudson and Colton."

"I appreciate your enthusiasm, but I don't want to go on a date tonight."

Easton looked troubled. "Do you *want* us to live with mom?"

"Of course not," Adam said. "Why would you even ask that question?"

His son lifted a shoulder. "It just seems like you're not doing everything you can to keep us."

He scrubbed his hands over his face again. "I really don't want you worrying about this, but I need you to know that nothing—*absolutely nothing*—is more important to me than you and your brothers, and I will do everything I can to keep you guys here with me."

"Forever?"

He managed a smile. "There might come a time when you want to move out, maybe to go to college or just to have a place of your own."

"No way," Easton said. "Morgan's Glen is the coolest place in the world."

"I think so, too," Adam agreed.

But it was obvious to Adam that his son was still worried, and he wasn't sure how to assuage his fears.

"But for now, can you please just trust that I'm the dad and I'm going to take care of things? You're the kid, you're supposed to focus on kid things like Pokémon and Mario and—" he glanced at the title of the book in his son's hand "—*Captain Underpants and the Terrifying Return of Tippy Tinkletrousers*."

Easton smiled at that, but his smile quickly faded.

"I'll try," he said. "But I don't like Greg."

Adam's parental radar quivered. The boys hadn't been out of his sight when they were with his ex-wife and her new husband, but still he felt compelled to ask Easton about it. "Did something happen in Las Vegas that made you feel uncomfortable?"

"He called me *pal*," Easton said. "I only just met the guy—I'm not his pal and I don't wanna be."

He exhaled a silent, shaky sigh of relief as his radar stopped quivering. "It might have been awkward for him, too," Adam allowed. "Meeting you and your brothers for the first time the day before he married your mom."

"That's not my fault."

"No," Adam agreed. "None of this is your fault."

"I wanna stay here," Easton said. "Why can't me and Hudson and Colton just tell the judge that we wanna stay here?"

"You might have an opportunity to do that, but I'm hoping that your mom and I can work things out between us so that we don't have to go in front of a judge." He drew in a bracing breath. "But that means you'll probably be spending more time with your mom—starting with Thanksgiving."

His son groaned. "We have to spend Thanksgiving with Mom?"

"No plans have been finalized yet," Adam said. "But I figure that if you go to your mom's for Thanksgiving, then it will be easier for me to argue that you should be here for Christmas."

"Of course we hafta be here for Christmas," Easton

said, sounding horrified by the prospect of being anywhere else.

It was a horrifying thought for Adam, too, and he vowed to do everything in his power to ensure that his greatest fears didn't become reality.

Chapter Ten

Olivia had a busy day Saturday, cleaning the house and then getting herself ready for her date with Leo. She painted her toenails and even shaved her legs, an admission—if only to herself—that she was contemplating the possibility of wrapping those legs around the good doctor later in the evening. Because it had been a really long time since she'd been naked with a man, and if there was going to be a fourth date, she wanted to know that they were physically compatible. Maybe it unnerved her a little to realize that watching a hockey game with Adam had stirred her up more than any of Leo's kisses, but there was no hope of anything happening with Adam and she refused to waste any more time thinking about him and wishing that things could be different.

After her shower, she considered and discarded various articles of clothing. If they were actually going out to The Home Station, a dress would be appropriate, but it seemed a little much for a quiet dinner at home. So she covered her brand-new sexy bra and underwear (thank you, Victoria!) with a soft knit V-neck tunic-style sweater and velvet leggings, then added silver hoop earrings and a circle-and-post pendant necklace, and spritzed on her favorite perfume.

Though she didn't know what would be on the menu for dinner, she figured that anything from the fanciest restaurant in town warranted her best place mats and linen napkins. So she set those out on the dining room table, then added candles in elegant silver holders and crystal wineglasses.

At six o'clock, she sent a text to Leo, asking for an ETA, and she opened a bottle of her favorite cabernet sauvignon, to allow it to breathe.

By six-fifteen, she hadn't received a response, so she poured a glass of wine.

At six thirty, she stared at the still blank screen on her phone and poured a second glass.

Adam wasn't in any hurry to go home after his meeting with Katelyn Gilmore. Needing some time to sort out the thoughts spinning in his brain, he decided to take a walk.

The lawyer had been reassuring. She'd promised him that she would do everything she could to ensure that Easton, Hudson and Colton stayed with him at Morgan's Glen, where they belonged. But she wouldn't make him any promises, reminding him that custody battles were never easy and there was no guarantee of the outcome.

"There are a lot of factors that weigh in your favor,"
she'd told him. "Not the least of which is that your sons
have always lived with you because your ex-wife chose
to leave them in your care. Because she trusted you to
meet their needs, and there's no evidence to suggest
that has changed."

No evidence except that his mom, who was a key
player in providing care for the boys, was having conversations with her dead husband and trekking out to
the mailbox in the middle of the night looking for letters from him.

His breath fogged in the frigid air, forcing him to acknowledge that even if he walked all night, he was more
likely to end up with frostbite than answers.

So he made his way back to his SUV and slid his key
into the ignition. As he cranked up the heat his stomach
growled, reminding him that it was well past dinnertime.

He considered Diggers'—where he could sit at the
bar to enjoy a burger and a beer. But Diggers' was likely
to be packed on a Saturday night, and he wasn't in
the mood to make conversation. Jo's was a better bet.
Though the local pizza place was likely to be just as
busy as the bar and grill, he could order some wings to
go and eat them in his car.

He was standing at the counter, waiting for his order,
when Olivia Gilmore walked in.

Their paths hadn't crossed since Vegas, but that
hadn't stopped him from thinking about her. Especially
after the kids were tucked into bed at night and the
house was so quiet that he turned on the television for
background noise. That was when he inevitably found
himself remembering how much he'd enjoyed talking

to her late into the night, how sweet she'd looked in her pj's and how good it had felt to hold her in his arms.

He'd been thinking about her so much that he'd actually considered stopping by the school to say "hi," but to what purpose? He'd been very clear that he didn't have the time for any kind of a romantic relationship and seeking her out might send a different signal.

"Miss Gilmore," he said.

"Olivia," she reminded him with a smile.

"Old habits," he said, with an apologetic shrug.

"No worries." She tucked her hands into her pockets. "So I guess the Morgans are having pizza for dinner tonight, too?"

"Actually, I'm waiting for wings and dining solo," he confided. "My mom made homemade mac and cheese for the boys."

"You're not a fan of mac and cheese?" she guessed.

"I had an appointment in town."

"With your lawyer," she guessed.

"How did you— Oh. Jamie," he realized.

She nodded. Then ventured cautiously to ask, "Everything okay?"

"No." His answer was blunt and probably more than a little rude. "How can everything be okay when I was served with papers suing for custody of my kids?"

She winced. "You're right. I'm sorry."

"No, I'm sorry," he said. "I shouldn't be taking my lousy mood out on you."

"No worries." She exchanged some bills for the flat, square box that was passed across the counter to her.

"What's on your pizza?" he asked.

"Pepperoni and hot peppers."

"There's an empty table in the corner," he said. "You want to share your pizza and my wings?"

"Oh. Um. Okay."

"Great. Why don't you grab— *Damn*," he said, as a couple of teens settled into the previously vacant chairs. "There *was* an empty table in the corner."

"There's an empty table at my house," she suggested as an alternative.

He hesitated, his brain scrambling. Because sharing a meal in a restaurant was safe; sharing a meal in Olivia's home, where they would be alone, seemed fraught with potential danger—or at least temptation.

"Adam?" she prompted.

"That sounds good to me," he said, confident that he could resist the allure of Olivia Gilmore.

Less than ten minutes later, he was walking through her front door. Though he'd never been in her town house before, the layout was almost identical to his sister's, one street over, with the front foyer leading to a center hallway with a living room/dining room combo on one side, a den/office and powder room on the other, kitchen at the back and bedrooms upstairs.

"You were expecting to share your pizza with someone else," he realized, eyeing the fancy dishes and candles on the dining room table.

"Actually, I was expecting to share something other than pizza with someone else," she told him.

"What happened?"

"Change of plans," she said.

Though her words were deliberately light, he thought he detected a hint of not just disappointment but hurt in her tone.

"And the wine?" He picked up the open bottle, already half-empty.

Her cheeks flushed. "I thought I'd have a glass while I was waiting. Then I had another. And then I decided I probably shouldn't be drinking on an empty stomach and ordered the pizza."

"Whoever he is, he's a fool."

"No, he's a doctor," she said, transferring a slice of pizza from the box to her plate.

"Ah." Adam added a few wings to the two slices already on his own plate. "How long have you been dating him?"

"We've had two dates in three months. Does that even count as dating?"

"Have you slept with him?" He held up a hand before she could respond. "No. Don't answer that. Better yet, let's pretend I didn't even ask such a totally inappropriate question."

"It was totally inappropriate," she agreed. "And the answer is no."

"None of my business," he assured her.

"Although I'd hoped to be able to give a different answer tomorrow."

"I'll bet if your doctor had known that, he wouldn't have let anything change his plans."

"He's not *my* doctor," Olivia said.

She poured some more wine into her glass, then offered the bottle to him. "Do you want some of this?"

"I'm not much of a wine drinker," he said. "Any chance you've got a beer in your fridge?"

"As a matter of fact." She pushed away from the table

and retreated to the kitchen, returning with a bottle of Wild Horse.

"Thanks."

"It's just so hard to meet someone," Olivia said, returning to her seat across from him. "Actually, that's not true. It's easy to meet someone—it's not easy to meet someone who's looking for something more than a casual hookup."

"I'll take your word for it," he said.

Olivia tipped the bottle over her glass again, frowning when she realized it was empty. "I guess you haven't dated much since the divorce."

"Not at all," he confirmed.

"So you just go for the casual hookup, too?"

"I don't… I mean… Can I plead the Fifth?"

She waved a hand dismissively. "This isn't a court of law and you're not on trial."

"Not yet, anyway."

"You're referring to Rebecca's application for custody," she ventured.

"It's hard to think about anything else," he admitted.

"She's not going to win," Olivia said confidently.

"You can't know that."

"I can," she insisted. "Because I know you, and I know Easton and Hudson and Colton, and no judge in his right mind would take those boys away from you."

"There's always the possibility that I could get a judge who's not in his right mind."

"Have some faith in the system. Or, if not the system, the fact that you've got a built-in support network in the form of your mom."

"Who might not be in her right mind."

Olivia frowned. "What?"

He shook his head. "Nothing."

"You know you can talk to me about anything, don't you?"

"Talking isn't going to help."

"How do you know?"

"Because I've been talking about it. I've talked to my sister and my mom and my lawyer. What I really want right now is to forget about it—even if only for five minutes."

"So what do you want to talk about?"

He shrugged. "Why don't you tell me about this doctor you're dating?"

"You mean the doctor I'm *not* dating and *not* having sex with?"

"Okay," he agreed cautiously.

She sighed. "Do you know how long it's been since I've had sex?"

"How would I possibly know something like that?" he asked, baffled—and intrigued.

"More than two years," she told him. "In fact, it's close to three years now. Since I went home with Bryan Jansen after the staff Christmas party." She sighed. "I was hoping we were going to have sex tonight."

Adam choked on his beer.

"Not you and me," she hastened to clarify. "Me and Leo."

He somehow managed to stop sputtering. "That's the doctor?"

She nodded. "I shaved my legs, bought sexy new underwear—a lacy demi-cup bra and matching—"

"Stop!"

She blinked at his vehement outburst. "What's wrong?"

"I realize you're just venting to me, as you would to one of your girlfriends. But I'm a man, and when you tell a man you're wearing sexy underwear, well, he can't help but picture you in that sexy underwear."

"Really?" She seemed surprised by his admission. "You're picturing me in my underwear?"

"Actually, I'm trying very hard not to."

"Hmm." Her eyebrows drew together as she considered his reluctant confession, then her lips slowly curved. "What color do you think they are?"

Black. Or red. Or white. Or—

"No," he said firmly. "We're *not* playing this game."

Her smile widened. "What color do you *wish* they were?"

"Olivia." Her name was a warning growl.

"Black," she told him, blatantly disregarding his warning. "With little pink bows here—" she touched the front of her sweater, between her breasts "—and—" then pointed to a spot just below where he imagined her belly button to be "—here."

And suddenly it was all too easy to picture her curvy body without the sweater and leggings, her delectable form clad in only scraps of black lace. Of course, his imagination was helped along by the fact that he'd seen her in a bathing suit, so he knew exactly how sexy she was. And the awareness that coursed through his veins was further enhanced by his recollection of dancing with her, and the memory of just how good she felt in his arms.

"I have to go." He abruptly pushed to his feet, picking up the mostly empty food boxes and carrying them to the kitchen.

She followed him with the plates, looking decidedly unhappy.

"There's something wrong with me, isn't there?" she said. "That's why Leo keeps standing me up and why you're practically racing out the door now?"

"There is absolutely nothing wrong with you," Adam told her. "The doctor, on the other hand, is obviously an idiot for not grabbing hold with both hands of what you're offering."

"Does that mean you're an idiot, too?" she challenged.

"Maybe," he allowed. "Or maybe I'm smart enough to know that if I took what you were offering right now, we'd both have regrets in the morning."

"I've always said that I'd rather regret something I did than something I didn't do." Then she grabbed the hem of her sweater with both hands and tugged it over her head, leaving her standing in front of him wearing heeled boots, velvet leggings and a black lace demi-cup bra with a little pink bow between her breasts, right where she'd indicated it would be.

He swore softly, reverently, as all the blood in his body migrated south.

Next she hooked her thumbs in the waistband of her leggings, and he knew that if he didn't get out of there—*now*—he wasn't going to leave before morning.

"GoodnightOlivia."

He tossed the words over his shoulder as he fled.

Olivia woke up Sunday morning with a raging hangover and the uncomfortable realization that she'd crossed a lot of lines with Adam Morgan the night before. Not that anything had actually happened, aside from the fact that she'd thrown herself at him—and fallen hard.

She wanted to pretend she hadn't made an overture, and she was pretty sure that Adam would let her. But she'd been raised to take responsibility for her actions, so she took a shower to clear the cobwebs from her brain, then put on her big-girl panties to clean up the mess she'd made.

When she stepped out of her vehicle at Morgan's Glen, she noticed that the barn door was ajar, so she headed their first.

"Adam?"

"Back here."

Following the direction of his voice, she found him in some kind of stockroom, unpacking a box of supplements.

"Hi," she said.

"Hello, Olivia."

Apparently all she'd had to do to get him to remember her given name was whip her sweater over her head and show him her breasts.

She licked her suddenly dry lips. "Are the boys in the house?"

"No, my mom took them to church and then to the comic book store in Battle Mountain."

"Oh."

"What brings you out this way on a Sunday morning?" he prompted.

"I wanted to apologize," she said, sincerely contrite.

"What exactly are you apologizing for?"

"Last night. For making things so…awkward." Her

cheeks burned as she recalled just how blatantly she'd thrown herself at him.

"Forget about it."

"I wish I could," she told him.

"That makes two of us," he muttered.

"I know I put you in a difficult position, and—"

"I said forget about it." The words were curt; his tone hard.

She felt the sting of tears at the back of her eyes. They'd been on the road to becoming friends, and she'd ruined it by letting herself hope—if only for a moment—that they might be more.

"That would be easier to do if you'd let me finish my apology."

"I don't want your apology. I want—" He cut himself off abruptly and dropped the hands that had started to reach for her. "I want you to go."

She turned away, willing to accede to his request. Unwilling to make an even bigger fool of herself than she'd already done.

"Olivia—wait."

"Make up your mind," she said, torn between weariness and frustration. "Do you want me to stay? Or do you want me to go?"

He sighed, sounding as weary as she felt. "You should go."

"That's not really an answer to my question," she noted. "I asked what *you* want."

"What I want…isn't the same thing you want."

"How do you know what I want?" she challenged.

"Because even if I hadn't already guessed that you

were a traditional kind of woman, you told me last night exactly what you want—a husband and a family."

"Last night, I wanted sex."

"And you very nearly got your wish," he muttered.

She stepped in front of him. "What do *you* want, Adam?"

A muscle in his jaw flexed, the only outward sign that he was aware of her presence as he kept his gaze resolutely fixed somewhere over her shoulder.

So she lifted a hand and laid it on his chest, making physical contact to remind him of her presence. To make him see her.

And it worked.

His gaze, blazing with heat and intensity, locked on her.

She had to swallow before she could speak, but no way was she going to back down.

"Tell me," she urged softly.

"You want to know what I want?" he challenged.

She nodded.

"I want *you*, Olivia. Naked in my bed. It's what I've wanted since the weekend we spent together in Vegas. It's what I've dreamed about every night since then."

She was taken aback by his unexpected admission— and deeply aroused.

"Then why did you leave last night?"

"Because we don't want the same things," he said again.

"Each of us wanting the other naked seems like the same thing to me."

He shook his head. "You want the intimacy of sex—I just need to get laid."

She didn't believe it. If that was all he wanted, he could have had it last night. She certainly wouldn't have objected.

"So maybe there's a way that we could each give the other what they want."

"How?" he challenged.

"By getting married."

Adam laughed, because he was certain that she had to be joking.

But the woman standing in front of him didn't even crack a smile. Instead, she just watched him, her expression equal parts hopeful and exasperated.

"I'll be the first to admit that I've been out of the game for a while," he said. "But back in the day, a man and a woman usually went on a couple of dates before they made an appointment with a justice of the peace."

"You're right," she decided. "We should probably go out, at least once or twice, to make our marriage more believable."

"I'm relieved to learn that you're proposing some kind of ruse, because I thought, for a moment, that you were actually proposing."

"I am," she insisted.

"Then I'm going to have to say *no*."

"Think about it," she urged. "Rebecca is claiming that she can offer the boys a more stable home because she's married. If you were married, too, her argument falls completely flat."

Obviously his sister had floated her marriage-as-a-solution-to-all-his-problems theory to her best friend, too.

"And what would you get out of this?" he asked.

"The family I've always wanted."

"And when you grow tired of the charade?"

"I'm not suggesting any kind of charade or temporary marriage," she said, sounding scandalized by the thought.

Now he was even more confused. "You can't honestly be suggesting a legal union, 'til death do us part."

"Why not?"

"Because, as was already noted, we haven't even been on a date. We barely know each other."

"We've known each other for more than twenty years."

"I'm not sure your lifelong friendship with my sister translates into any kind of connection between you and me."

"And we spent the better part of forty-eight hours together in Vegas," she reminded him. "We talked. We laughed. We danced."

He still looked skeptical.

"There was a moment," she insisted. "Don't you dare deny it."

"There was a moment in which I contemplated the potential benefits of us in bed together," he acknowledged. "Before I remembered all the reasons it would be a bad idea."

"Which proves there's an attraction."

"I've been attracted to a lot of women and not, for a single minute, been tempted to marry any of them."

"It's understandable that your divorce would make you wary."

"I'm not wary," he denied. "I simply refuse to make the same mistake twice."

"I would never walk out on my husband and children," she told him. "And if we were married, your sons would be mine, too, in every way that matters."

"That all sounds well and good," he said. "But Rebecca actually *is* their mother, and she still left."

"Which is why you need a wife—a mother figure for your children. I'm not underestimating the role your mom has played in their lives. But she's their grandmother, not their mother."

He couldn't deny that there was some truth in what she was saying. And he'd seen it himself when they were in Las Vegas, the way his sons had clamored for Olivia's attention and sought her validation—and got it, too. He didn't feel threatened by their obvious affection for his sister's best friend, because he knew that his position in their lives was secure. They weren't seeking a new parental figure but specifically looking for a mom.

"I don't think you know enough about my family to be in any position to tell me what we need," he said.

"I know that nothing is more important to you than your family," Olivia said. "Closely followed by Morgan's Glen. I also know that you haven't been involved with anyone since Rebecca left. Maybe you go into Elko or Battle Mountain when you want to hook up with someone and not worry about running into her at The Daily Grind the next day—I don't know and I don't need to know any of the details," she assured him. "But if we were to go ahead with this plan, I would like to know that you haven't been having unprotected sex."

"You didn't express any concerns about that last night," he felt compelled to point out to her.

"Because there's a box of condoms in my bedside table," she said. "But I'm also on the pill, so if we were married, we could dispense with the extra layer of protection."

"I can't believe we're even having this conversation."

"My mother always told me that if I couldn't talk to a man about sex, I shouldn't even think about getting naked with him."

"And mine told me that I shouldn't ever have sex with a woman I wasn't willing to marry, because the only form of birth control that's one-hundred-percent effective is abstinence." His mouth twisted in a wry smile. "She was right."

"I think we're getting sidetracked a little here," Olivia said.

"Maybe," he allowed. "But now you've got me wondering—do *you* go to Elko or Battle Mountain when you want a quick tumble between the sheets?"

Her cheeks burned. "I don't need to go out of town," she said indignantly. "I have a trusty little handheld device that goes as long as I need it to."

"Maybe I should be intimidated, but I find myself intrigued," he confided.

"And now we're way off topic," she said.

"I don't think we are," he disagreed. "Because if you're serious about this marriage idea, especially about it not being temporary, it would be smart to test our… compatibility, don't you think?"

"I offered you that opportunity last night," she reminded him.

"You were under the influence last night. And wearing sexy underwear that you'd put on in the hope that another man would take it off you."

"So you're a gentleman?"

"But not a saint." He took another step toward her. "Are you clearheaded today?"

She nodded.

"Good," he said.

And then he kissed her.

He'd only wanted an answer to the question that plagued him: What would it be like to kiss her? But he knew right away that he'd made a tactical error. Because that first touch of his lips to hers released a torrent of need inside him.

Her mouth was every bit as soft as he'd imagined; her flavor even more intoxicating than he'd anticipated. And, yes, he'd spent a lot of time thinking about kissing her since Vegas. And a lot of time reminding himself that there were a whole bunch of reasons that it would be a mistake to act upon the attraction he felt for his sister's best friend.

None of those reasons mattered now.

Nothing mattered but how good it felt to finally hold her in his arms, to feel her curves pressed against him, to taste the sweetness of the mouth that opened willingly for him.

He vaguely registered a sound in the distance—one that he should have recognized as the barn door sliding open. But he was so caught up in finally kissing Olivia that it took a few seconds for the pieces to click together in his brain, and those few seconds were apparently long enough for his sons to make their way down to the supply room, because the next thing he heard was Easton saying, "Dad—why are you kissing Miss Gilmore?"

Chapter Eleven

Olivia said a quick "hello" and "goodbye" to Easton, Hudson and Colton and made a hasty escape, leaving Adam to answer their questions. Because she had no doubt they'd have more questions than the one that Easton had already asked to interrupt the sizzling kiss she'd been enjoying with his dad.

It was always embarrassing to be caught in a compromising position, but to be caught in a lip-lock by Adam's children—one of whom was a student in her class!—was beyond awkward. As she drove away from the ranch, she felt certain that her cheeks would never stop burning.

Of course, her cheeks weren't the only part of her burning, and she couldn't help but wonder how far things might have gone if they hadn't been interrupted.

She'd been home less than ten minutes when a dark

SUV pulled into her driveway. Looking out the front window, her silly heart leaped inside her chest as she let herself imagine—for that brief second before the driver's door opened and an unfamiliar figure got out— that Adam had followed her back to town to tell her that he'd changed his mind about her proposal.

Or that he at least wanted to finish what they'd started.

But it wasn't Adam.

It was a delivery person with an enormous bouquet of yellow, red and purple flowers in a tall cylindrical vase.

"Olivia Gilmore?" the man asked when she opened the door.

"That's me," she confirmed.

He handed her the flowers. "Have a nice day."

"Thank you."

She set the vase on the coffee table and pulled the card out of the envelope.

I'm so sorry about last night, and I know I've given you too many excuses and not enough flowers, so hopefully these will help restore some balance.
XO Leo

She sank down onto the edge of the sofa and buried her face in her hands. She'd completely forgotten about Leo!

How could she have forgotten about Leo?

She'd been upset about being stood up again the previous night, but truth be told, as soon as she'd seen Adam at Jo's, she'd forgotten about her aborted plans with the doctor. At least until she and Adam had come back to her house and he'd commented on the candles and wine on the table.

Should she feel guilty?

Obviously Leo did, if the gorgeous arrangement of roses, asters, carnations and chrysanthemums was any indication.

But really, he had no reason to feel guilty. She understood that a doctor's patients would always be his priority. And while he'd probably been busy at the hospital again today, following up on last night's surgeries, she'd been making out with Adam Morgan.

She pulled her phone out of the side pocket of her purse and accessed his contact information.

The flowers are gorgeous—thank you.

She didn't expect a quick reply to her text message and was startled when her phone immediately rang. And again when she glanced at the screen and saw the caller identified as Leo Delissio.

She swiped to connect the call. "Hi."

"I'm so sorry," Leo said in lieu of a greeting.

"You already said that on the card."

"I feel as if I can't say it enough times," he told her. "I really wasn't supposed to be on call last night, but there was a multivehicle pileup north of Battle Mountain and more patients in need of treatment than Dr. Shah could handle."

And yet, he'd taken the time to think of her and send her flowers.

He really was a good guy.

Unfortunately, he wasn't the guy she wanted.

"You don't need to explain," Olivia said. "If I was ever under the mistaken impression that doctors worked regular hours, I'm not anymore."

She heard his name echo in the background.

Leo sighed. "I'm being paged."

"Go," she said. "But thank you again…"

She didn't bother to finish, because he was already gone.

"I've learned something interesting this year," Jamie remarked to Olivia while they were having lunch together in the teachers' lounge Monday.

"What's that?" she asked, unwrapping her sandwich.

"Fourth-grade boys gossip as much as girls."

"And what was the hot topic of conversation today?" Olivia asked, because it was obvious that her friend wanted to tell her.

"Easton's dad kissing Miss Gilmore."

Olivia felt her cheeks grow hot. "It's not what you think."

"So you didn't kiss my brother?" Jamie pressed.

"*He* kissed *me*."

Her friend's eyebrows lifted. "Are you saying that you didn't kiss him back?"

"I'm saying that he initiated it."

After she'd first propositioned and then proposed to him, though she didn't offer that information to her longtime friend.

"Well, you must have initiated *something*," Jamie decided. "Because according to Easton, you were caught together in the barn at Morgan's Glen."

"I went to the ranch to talk to Adam," she admitted. "About what we were talking about last week."

"You're referring to Rebecca's custody application?"

She nodded. "And your suggestion that he level the playing field."

"I'm not sure I'm following."

"I suggested to Adam that we should get married."

"I wasn't really suggesting that he should get married," her friend protested. "Or maybe I was—because he would be absolutely devastated if he lost those boys. But I certainly wasn't suggesting that he should marry you."

"You'd rather he picked some random woman from an online dating site whose profile says that she loves the outdoors and wants to have a family, but doesn't really have the first clue about what it means to live on a ranch or be a mom?"

"Of course not," Jamie said. "I'd rather he fell in love with someone who would love Easton, Hudson and Colton as much as she loves him."

"Why can't that be me?" Olivia challenged.

"I'm not saying it couldn't be. But I have to wonder..." Jamie trailed off, nibbling on her bottom lip.

"What are you wondering?"

"If you're maybe going down this path...because I just got engaged."

Olivia was stunned. And maybe a little hurt.

"Is that really what you think? That I'm trying to race you down the aisle?"

"No," Jamie said quickly, though her denial was immediately followed by an amendment. "I don't know. I guess I'm just feeling blindsided by all of this."

"Well, it doesn't matter, anyway," Olivia told her. "Because Adam turned down my offer."

"Before or after the kiss?" her friend asked curiously.

"Before *and* after," she admitted.

"Just one more question," Jamie said.

"What's that?" she asked warily.

"If he'd already turned down your offer…then what was the purpose of the kiss?"

Olivia wished she had an answer to that question, because if she knew why Adam had kissed her, she'd know how to get him to kiss her again.

For as far back as Adam could remember, his mom had always done a big meal to celebrate Thanksgiving: an enormous turkey with homemade-sausage-and-sage stuffing, mashed potatoes, gravy and half a dozen vegetables that she insisted he take at least a spoonful of each. Of course, he always did so to make her happy, and then he filled the rest of his plate with turkey, stuffing and potatoes.

When Adam and Rebecca got married, his mom had been careful not to step on her new daughter-in-law's toes, asking if the newlyweds wanted to join them for the traditional meal or celebrate on their own. Rebecca had jumped at the chance to eat with his parents rather than tackle the cooking of a turkey. And so his family's tradition had become their tradition, too.

When his dad died, it was only a few weeks before Thanksgiving and Adam had been certain that his mom would want to skip the festivities that year. He'd protested that it was too much work, but she wouldn't be dissuaded, insisting that a tradition was a tradition for a reason. Plus, she already had the turkey in her freezer.

So every year when they sat down together for the big meal, Adam said a prayer of thanks for his family. But this year was going to be different, and he wasn't looking forward to it. The holiday simply wouldn't be the same without his boys and he didn't have it in him to pretend otherwise.

But Easton, Hudson and Colton weren't the only ones who would be missing from their Thanksgiving gathering this year. His newly engaged sister and her fiancé were making the trip to Portland to spend the long weekend with Thomas's family.

Still, as much as Adam wasn't looking forward to Thanksgiving this year, he was cautiously optimistic that this would be his first *and* last holiday without his sons at the table. He was still trying to figure out what Rebecca's endgame was, why she was suddenly pretending that she wanted to be a full-time mom, but he figured it would pass.

And while he'd tried to put a positive spin on the change of plans for Easton, Hudson and Colton, they had *not* been happy. Mostly they'd been worried about missing out on Gramma's pumpkin pie, so she'd promised to make an extra one, just for them to enjoy when they came home.

Later, Adam had assured his mom that she only needed to make one that they would have when the boys returned. That was when Shirley told him that she'd accepted an invitation for both of them to celebrate the holiday with Angela Gilmore's family.

He had no intention of being dragged along, but he

couldn't say no to his mom. Or maybe he didn't try too hard to wiggle out of the obligation, because he was fairly certain that Charles and Angela's daughter would be at their table for the holiday meal. He hadn't seen Olivia since the day he'd kissed her, but he hadn't been able to stop thinking about that kiss.

And now he was pulling into the long drive leading to the various homesteads that were part of the Circle G. Jack Gilmore—the patriarch of the family—lived on the property with his wife, Evelyn, as did their sons David and Charles, and their wives. There was a third son, Robert, who'd moved out to California years ago, and whose youngest daughter, Haylee, had recently moved to Haven—and married Trevor Blake.

Adam wasn't clear on all the details of the feud between the Gilmores and the Blakes, but he knew that its roots were long and deep. Still, it seemed as though the two families had managed to bury the hatchet in recent years, as evidenced by the fact that Caleb Gilmore—one of David's sons—had his own home on the ranch with his wife, Brielle, whose mother was a Blake.

There were a lot of cars already parked in the driveway by the time Adam and Shirley arrived, tempting Adam to turn his vehicle around and drive away again. But as much as he wasn't looking forward to sitting around the table with a bunch of strangers, he knew that this was where his mom wanted to be, so here they were.

"We're so happy you could join us," Charles said, greeting them at the door.

"Thank you for having us," Adam said, inwardly cringing at the stilted sound of his own voice.

"It's our pleasure," Angela said warmly, kissing both of his cheeks.

Olivia made her way to the foyer then, offering his mom a hug and Adam a warm smile, apparently feeling no awkwardness to be sharing the holiday with the man who'd had his tongue down her throat only four days earlier. But there was definitely awareness sizzling in the air between them, so tangible he was surprised that no one else seemed to notice it.

"Are those pumpkin pies you've got there, Shirley?" Charles asked, the question interrupting Adam's prurient fantasies.

"They certainly are," she confirmed.

"Let me take them for you," he offered.

"Into the kitchen," his wife said firmly.

"Where else would I take them?" he asked, feigning innocence.

"The den, maybe, to hide them in the bottom drawer of your desk."

"Why don't I take the pies to the kitchen while you get drinks for our guests?" Olivia said, stealing the tray from her dad.

"That's a good idea," Angela agreed.

"I snuck away with half a pie—*once*," Charles confided to Adam. "And I've been treated like a criminal in my own home ever since."

"Come on," Olivia said, gesturing for Adam to follow her. "I'll introduce you to everyone."

Of course, he already knew her brothers, Michael and Mitchell, and though he vaguely remembered Mitch's wife, Lindsay, from their days at Westmount

High, he knew her better now as Elliott and Avenlea's mom, because Elliott was one of Hudson's best friends.

He was introduced to Marissa and Antonio—Olivia's cousin and her husband—their infant daughter, Seraphina, and a man named Chester.

"Call me Chip. Please," the cowboy said, as Angela called everyone to take their places around the table.

Dinner at the Gilmores was…nice, Adam decided, as platters and bowls were passed around the table.

Being a father to three active boys, he was no stranger to chaos, but the Gilmores seemed to take it up another notch. Or maybe it was the fact that there were fourteen of them seated, practically shoulder-to-shoulder, around the table.

"Of course, the baby doesn't actually need a chair," Olivia had confided as she slid into the seat beside him. "But my mom would never set the table for thirteen, because she believes it's bad luck."

He was glad the baby wouldn't eat any pie, because his mom had only made four—and she'd left one of those at home for Easton, Hudson and Colton.

"Sweet potatoes?"

"Huh?"

He turned to see Olivia offering him a spoonful of the mashed orange vegetable with some kind of crumbly nut topping.

"Um. No, thanks. I'm not really a fan of—"

But she was already putting a spoonful of the orange vegetable onto his plate.

"You're not a fan because you haven't tried *my* sweet potatoes," she told him.

There were lots of things of hers he wanted to try, but sweet potatoes weren't anywhere on the list.

She paused in the act of dipping the serving spoon into the casserole dish again. "You're not allergic to nuts, are you?"

"Shouldn't you have asked that question before you put them on my plate?"

Her cheeks colored prettily. "Yes, I should have."

"No, I'm not allergic to nuts."

"Good." She passed the bowl to her sister-in-law, seated on his other side.

Through bits and pieces of the conversation that flowed as freely as the wine being poured around the table, Adam learned that Chip was a ranch hand at the Circle G. Apparently the cowboy didn't have any family, so he was regularly invited to celebrate the holidays with Charles and Angela, or David and Valerie. As a result, he seemed well-acquainted with most everyone around the table, though it seemed to Adam that he took a particular interest in Olivia.

Not that he could blame the other man, but still, he didn't like it. Nor did he like the fact that she seemed happy to give the cowboy the attention he sought.

After everyone had eaten their fill, plates were cleared, and coffee and tea were served.

Olivia accepted the offer of a "special coffee" and was handed a cup topped with whipped cream and caramel drizzle.

"What else is in that, besides coffee?" Adam asked curiously.

"Cream, sugar and a very generous splash of amaretto."

"You might need to hitch a ride back into town with your brother after you drink that."

"I'm not going back into town tonight," she confided. "I'll spend the night here, in my old bedroom, and tomorrow morning, I'll be up early to help mom get started on the Christmas baking. It's one of our favorite holiday traditions."

Adam and his boys had a lot of holiday traditions, too. Traditions that might be in jeopardy if Rebecca was successful in her application for custody—which was definitely *not* something he wanted to think about right now."

"I need to stretch my legs," he said. "Do you think anyone will mind if I slip away for a few minutes?"

"Of course not," Olivia said. "Do you want some company?"

"Actually, I do," he replied.

"So what's the story with you and the cowboy?" he asked, after they'd unearthed their coats from the pile of garments on the hooks at the back door and ventured out into the cold, dark night.

"Chip?"

"Yeah."

"There's no story."

"Are you sure? Because your mom seemed to be nudging you two together and he certainly seemed interested."

"My mom nudges me toward any single man who crosses her path," she confided.

"And you resist all of her efforts?" he guessed.

"Actually, I don't," she said, surprising him with her response. "But so far, her efforts haven't been any more successful than my own."

"So why are you out here with me rather than inside with him?"

"Because you looked like you needed a friend—and while Chip is a really nice guy, there is absolutely zero chemistry between us."

"I wouldn't put too much stock in chemistry," he said. "Sure, the sparks might seem like fun in the beginning, until the sparks lead to a fire that incinerates every aspect of your life, and the next thing you know, you're at a stranger's Thanksgiving table without your kids."

"I realize you might not consider me a friend, but I thought I was a step up from a stranger," she said, sounding hurt.

"I'm sorry. You are. Of course you are. I'm just having a tough time today. This is the first major holiday that I've celebrated without the boys."

"I'm sorry."

"My only consolation is if Rebecca stays true to form, it will be my first and last holiday without them."

Olivia opened her mouth as if to say something, then closed it again without uttering a sound.

"Go on," he said. "Say whatever it is you wanted to say."

"It's really none of my business."

"I'm not going to disagree with that, but you obviously have an opinion."

Her lips twitched. "I'm a teacher," she reminded him. "I have opinions about everything."

"So tell me what you think," he urged.

"I think it's a lot colder out here than I realized," she said, muscling open the door of the barn and leading him inside.

The scent of hay and horses was familiar and surprisingly soothing. She paused at each stall to murmur a few words to its equine resident and offer a treat.

"You're a sweet-potato pusher," he said, when he realized what she was giving them.

"Tell me my sweet-potato casserole wasn't delicious," she challenged.

"It was good," he admitted, following her through a door labeled "tack room."

He immediately saw that it was a lot more than that, the generous space doing double duty as a lounge. On one side, saddles, bridles, bits and blankets were meticulously organized on hangers, hooks and in cubbies, with plenty of padded bench seating available. The other side had an overstuffed leather sofa and chairs arranged around a mission-style coffee table, facing a river-rock gas fireplace with a flat-screen TV mounted above the mantel. Unsurprising, the scents of leather and saddle soap prevailed here, underscored by a quiet whisper of wealth.

Adam prided himself on keeping all of his buildings and equipment in good repair, but while his tack room was neat, it wasn't anything like this.

Olivia immediately moved toward the seating area, picking up a remote from the coffee table and punching a couple of buttons. Suddenly flames were flickering behind the glass grate, adding a soft glow of light and warmth to the room.

"That's better," she said, rubbing her hands together in front of the fire.

"Now tell me what you were going to say about Rebecca's custody application," he urged.

She shrugged out of her coat and tossed it over the arm of one of the chairs. "I was only going to say that it's good for the boys to have a relationship with their mom. I know they've got wonderful female role models in their aunt and their grandma, but the absence of a parent in a child's life can have lasting repercussions."

"Isn't it just as important for children to have a stable home environment?"

"Absolutely," she agreed.

"Well, their lives have been stable." Following her example, he removed his coat and set it beside hers. "Until two weeks ago."

"I don't think their lives were upended by their mother's wedding. And regardless of what might or might not happen with her custody application, your boys are going to be just fine because they know their dad is always going to be in their corner."

"I don't want to talk about this anymore."

"Okay," she agreed easily. "What do you want to talk about?"

"I don't want to talk at all," he said, drawing her into his arms instead.

Chapter Twelve

Adam's mouth was hot and hungry when it captured hers, and Olivia responded with just as much heat and hunger. He'd warned her against trusting chemistry, but there was no denying that when she was close to him, something sparked. Something powerful and maybe even a little bit dangerous.

His hands were on her now, his touch adding fuel to the fire that burned inside her. For him. Only for him. She fisted her hands in his sweater, holding on to him as the world spun. When his tongue traced the seam of her lips, she parted them willingly. When he eased her back onto the sofa, she was more than willing. She was eager. Desperate.

There was so much heat between them that she was certain all the bones in her body had melted. Even her brain had gone to mush. She could think of nothing but Adam, want nothing but Adam.

"I should never have kissed you last week."

The words were muttered against her lips, and she might have taken offense to them if not for the fact that he was still touching her, still kissing her.

"I can tell you're full of regrets."

He chuckled softly as his hands slid beneath the hem of her sweater. "You make me crazy, Liv."

"Sanity is overrated."

"Let's get rid of this," he suggested, lifting the hem of her sweater and whisking it over her head, revealing her red lace bra. He sucked in a breath. "You. Are. So. Damn. Sexy."

Sexy wasn't a word she ever would have used to describe herself. But the way Adam was looking at her now, she felt sexy. Desirable.

Desired.

"I need to touch you."

She shivered as his callused palms moved over her torso, the rough texture scraping lightly over her tender skin, making her shiver.

"I want you to touch me."

The tight peaks of her nipples pressed against the lacy fabric of her bra, practically begging for his attention.

Her breath caught as his thumbs skimmed over her breasts, tracing circles around her nipples until she was almost whimpering with want, with need. She *did* whimper when his hands dropped away from her breasts, and he responded with a wicked smile before he lowered his head and took one of the taut, aching peaks into his mouth.

She gasped, then moaned, as he laved and suckled, causing arrows of heat to spear toward her center.

He shifted his attention to her other breast, showing it the same careful attention, until she was practically writhing beneath him. Then he unhooked the front fastening of her bra and peeled back the cups, baring her breasts to his gaze, his hands, his mouth.

Desperate to touch him, too, she slid her hands beneath the hem of his sweater, whimpering with frustration when she encountered another layer of fabric instead of skin. He pulled away from her only long enough to yank the sweater and T-shirt over his head, then he was kissing her again.

She was more than ready to surrender to the desire that thrummed in her veins, and she ran her hands over the smooth, hard muscles of his chest, feeling them tense and ripple in response to her touch. Even through the layers of denim, she could feel his erection pressing into her, and she lifted her hips off the sofa to rub her pelvis against his, making him groan.

"If we don't stop now, we're not going to," he warned.

"I don't want to stop."

He was the last man she should be considering an affair with. He was her best friend's brother. The father of one of her students.

He was also her first real crush.

The only man who'd made her heart beat faster with a smile.

Who made her knees quiver when he was close.

She'd been certain she would outgrow her crush.

She'd dated other guys. She'd had other lovers. But she'd never felt about anyone the way she felt about

Adam Morgan. And there was no way she was going to walk away from him now.

Her desire for him wasn't at all reasonable.

It wasn't the least bit rational.

But it was undeniable.

He tugged off her boots and tossed them aside, then pulled her jeans down her legs and discarded those, too, leaving her clad in a pair of scarlet bikini panties.

"So. Damn. Sexy," he said again.

Then he lowered his head between her thighs and licked her through the thin fabric barrier. Her hips instinctively lifted, and he slid his hands beneath her buttocks, holding her in place so that he could feast on her.

The pleasure came fast, not just a wave but a tsunami, battering at her from all directions, crashing over her, again and again, long after she was certain she couldn't survive any more.

"Condom." The word was a desperate, breathless plea.

He held up a square packet.

Obviously the man believed in being prepared, for which she was very grateful.

She took the packet from him while he quickly discarded his jeans and socks, leaving him clad in only a pair of black knit boxers.

"Looks like you've got something else for me," she said, sliding a hand into his shorts to wrap her fingers around his erection, making him groan.

"It is, indeed, for you," he assured her.

"In that case—" she drew her hand away so that she could hook both hands in the waistband of his boxers and draw them down his legs, dropping to her knees in front of him as she did so "—I'm going to take it out and play with it."

"Careful," he warned. "It's been a long time since... Ooohh."

She licked him, letting her tongue trace along his length from base to tip. Her lips curved in a smile as she felt the muscles in his thighs tremble, as she gave back at least some of the pleasure he'd already given to her.

But when she started to take him in her mouth, he fisted his hand in her hair and gently drew her head back.

"Condom."

This time he was the one who spoke, his voice hoarse, strained.

She carefully opened the square packet and slowly unrolled the latex over his rigid shaft. Then she drew him back down onto the sofa, wrapping her arms and legs around him. He kissed her hard and deep then, and he took her body the same way.

And it felt good. So...good.

Having been so thoroughly sated already, she didn't expect the merging of their bodies to be anything more than a pleasurable experience. But with every thrust, he stoked her desire anew, pushing her closer and closer to the edge again. Harder. Faster.

Her head fell back against the padded arm of the sofa and her fingers dug in to his shoulders, holding on to him as pleasure continued to build inside her until it was almost more than she could bear. But still there was more.

And then...finally...release.

She cried out as her body convulsed around him, and

he captured her mouth again, swallowing her cries as the aftereffects of her orgasm continued to wrack her body until he groaned deeply and finally yielded to his own climax.

Being with Adam wasn't anything like she'd imagined.

Her fantasies had been romantic, perhaps even innocent.

The reality had been raw and powerful. More intense than anything she'd ever experienced, almost more than she could bear.

As he pulled a couple of tissues out of the box on the table to dispose of the condom, she turned away from him to gather her clothes. She didn't know why, but as she began to dress, she felt more exposed than when she'd been completely naked in his arms.

Was it regret?

She didn't think so, because how could she be sorry when her body was still humming with the aftereffects of pleasure?

But her fingers were unsteady, making her fumble with the hooks as she attempted to refasten her bra.

Sensing her struggles, Adam brushed her hands away to complete the task for her.

She managed a smile, though she felt it wobble a little around the edges. "Thanks."

"Are you okay?" he asked, sounding concerned. "Did I hurt you?"

"Yes. No." She shoved her arms into the sleeves of her sweater, then tugged it over her head. "Yes, I'm okay. No, you didn't hurt me."

"So why are you acting weird now?"

"Because I feel weird," she admitted.

"You think what just happened was a mistake," he guessed.

"No. But I do think it shouldn't have happened."

"Because your parents and my mom are in the house, less than two hundred feet away?"

"Believe it or not, their proximity doesn't even crack the top three reasons."

"What are those reasons?"

"Number one is that you're my best friend's brother. Number two is that you're the parent of one of my students."

"And number three?" he prompted.

"What?"

"You said there were three reasons more significant than the proximity of our respective parents."

Number three is that I've been in love with you since I was fifteen, and there's no way I'm ever going to get over my crush now.

But she had no intention of saying *that* aloud.

"I guess the folks are number three," she said instead.

"Well, to deal with your concerns in order—I have no intention of telling my sister that I had sex with her best friend and I promise not to bring up what happened here at the next Stoney Ridge open house."

"Or the upcoming holiday concert?"

"Or the upcoming holiday concert," he agreed.

She attempted another smile.

He lifted a hand and brushed his thumb over her bottom lip, still swollen from his kisses.

"I was just thinking…if we got married, you wouldn't have to feel guilty about having sex with me."

"If we were married, we also wouldn't have to have sex in the tack room."

"But we could if we wanted to, right?" he said with a wink.

She laughed at that.

"Is it a little less weird now?"

"I don't know," she said. "But I don't feel guilty and I don't have regrets."

"Good." He kissed her then, long and slow and deep. "Thanks for giving me something to be thankful for this Thanksgiving."

"It was my pleasure."

"The pleasure was very definitely mutual."

Shirley had been a little apprehensive about spending Thanksgiving at the Circle G. Though she and Angela Gilmore had been friends for a long time, they'd never spent the holidays together before because each of them was busy with their own family. Her friend was busy with her family this year, too, but Angela had thoughtfully invited Shirley and Adam to join them, knowing that they would otherwise be on their own.

And it had been an enjoyable meal. A little more chaotic than what she was accustomed to—even with three rowdy grandsons in the house—but enjoyable. Now the tables had been cleared and the leftovers put away, and Shirley and Angela were sitting by the fire in the living room, savoring coffee spiked with amaretto, while Charles, MG and Chip washed the dishes and tidied up the kitchen.

"You've got your men well-trained," Shirley noted.

"They are good about helping with the cleanup," Angela acknowledged. "Of course, Mitch had an excuse to duck out, because Elliott and Avenlea were tired and he and Lindsay wanted to get them home to bed before they got cranky."

"Lindsay looked just as tired as the kids."

"I was always exhausted, too, in the early stages of pregnancy," Angela confided.

"Really? They're going to have another baby? I can't believe nobody mentioned it at dinner."

"They haven't even told me and Charles yet," her friend admitted. "But I know they've been trying, and I recognize the signs."

"You're going to have another grandchild." Shirley was thrilled for her friend, aware that Angela doted on Elliott and Avenlea as much as she did on Easton, Hudson and Colton.

"Before summer, if my guess is correct," Angela said.

"And I've got a summer wedding to look forward to—and hopefully another grandbaby not too long after that."

"Olivia told me about Jamie's engagement. You must be so excited."

"I am, of course. Thomas is a good man who obviously adores her, and I feel confident that they're going to be very happy together." Her sigh was wistful. "I just wish that Adam had been as lucky in love."

"His marriage might not have worked out, but it gave him three adorable boys."

"Who are with their mom and her new husband today instead of with their dad."

"Lucky for him, he has a wonderful mother who got him out of the house."

"To be honest, it wasn't as tough to sell as I thought it might be," Shirley confided.

"He probably realized that it would be easier to spend the day away from home, where the boys' absence wouldn't be so glaringly obvious."

"I'm sure that was part of it. But I think another part was the prospect of seeing Olivia."

"There did seem to be a little bit of a spark between them," Angela noted.

"So why did you seat her next to that handsome cowboy at dinner?"

"Adam was seated on her other side."

"So that he couldn't help but notice that the other man was interested," Shirley mused.

"I thought he might need a little nudge in the right direction."

"I'd do more than nudge, if I thought it would do any good. But he's so focused on his responsibilities—to the boys and the ranch. And while I know his sons are a great source of joy, he needs more. He needs a partner to share his life. Someone who makes the long winter nights seem not so long—or at least not so lonely. And the way he was looking at Olivia tonight, I really think she could be that someone."

"I can't imagine anything that would make her happier," Angela said. "Though she's never admitted it in so many words, I know she's been in love with Adam for a long time, and no matter how many other men she's dated, there's never been anyone else for her."

"It would make me happy, too, to know that my son had found a woman who loved him as he deserves to be loved. But..."

"But what?" her friend prompted.

"But if we're wrong, one or both of our children could end up with a broken heart."

"And if we're right, and I truly believe that we are," Angela said, "then we'll be in the front seats to witness their happiness."

Shirley held up her cup in the gesture of a toast. "And maybe there will be more grandchildren in both of our futures."

Chapter Thirteen

He'd had sex with Olivia Gilmore.

His sister's best friend.

Hudson's teacher.

Not just sex, but hot sweaty sex in the barn.

Maybe he should be ashamed of the fact that he'd finally succumbed to his desire for her while their respective families were still seated around the dinner table inside the house. But right now, remembering that she'd been as eager for him as he was for her, Adam wasn't feeling anything but completely satisfied.

Unfortunately, thinking about the softness of her skin, the sweetness of her kiss and the warmth of her body was enough to churn him up all over again. So he pushed the memories out of his mind, but then he was faced with the realization that his house was too quiet.

Because the boys weren't home, and he missed them every single minute while they were gone.

Well, maybe not during the time that he'd been in the tack room with Olivia.

While he was there, he hadn't been thinking of anyone but her.

But since he'd come home to his empty house, their absence had loomed large. Easton and Hudson were both old enough now to attend the occasional sleepover at a friend's house, but they'd never been away overnight at the same time, and he'd certainly never been home with all three of them gone.

Sure, he'd spent the odd night away when he'd gone to a cattle auction out of town, but he'd always known that the boys were safe at home with his mom.

He trusted that they were safe with Rebecca, too. She wasn't always reliable, but he knew that she wouldn't ever let any harm come to their boys. So it wasn't that he was worried about them, but that they weren't where they were supposed to be—in their beds under his roof, where he could tuck them in, kiss them good-night and then check on them again before he went to his own bed.

It was a normal part of his routine, so automatic that he didn't need to think about it. And when he'd stood at the threshold of Hudson and Colton's room the night before and suddenly remembered that they weren't there, tucked snugly in their beds with their favorite stuffed toys around them, their absence had been like a spear to his heart.

It's good for the boys to have a relationship with their mom.

Olivia was right, and he'd always encouraged Rebecca

to visit whenever she wanted. She was the one who'd chosen to be absent from their lives, and they'd gotten used to that status quo. Now, suddenly, she'd changed her mind and thrown everything into a tailspin.

And until the custody issue was decided—*again*— his lawyer had advised him to play nice. So he'd spent the morning after Thanksgiving doing what he always did—taking care of the cattle and horses and checking for any problems with the fence or signs of predators… and trying not to think of what his boys were doing.

He wanted them to have a good time, but he didn't want them to have such a good time that they'd decide it would be more fun to live with Mom than with Dad.

Any concerns he had were alleviated when Greg's truck pulled into the driveway and they tumbled out of the vehicle to race toward him, and their hugs went a long way toward soothing the ache in his heart.

"Thanks for bringing them home," he said to their stepdad, as the boys headed into the house to see their grandmother—and dig in to the promised pie.

"Not a problem," Greg assured him. "I'm heading into Battle Mountain for a meeting, so it was on my way."

"You have meetings today?"

"Working in finance is like ranching—there are no days off."

"Except you don't have to worry about stepping in cow manure in a boardroom," Adam said, looking pointedly at the man's shiny loafers.

"But I do have to wade through a lot of BS."

The response surprised a laugh out of Adam. "I think I'd rather stick with raising cattle."

"Good call," Greg said. Then, "Did you have a good Thanksgiving?"

Yes. Because he'd had sex. Mind-blowingly hot sex with an amazing and passionate woman.

No. Because he'd missed his kids unbearably.

Except when he was in the barn having the aforementioned mind-blowingly hot sex. Because as much as he loved his boys, they'd been the furthest thing from his mind at that point in time.

"It was pretty quiet," he said.

Except when he'd had to cover Olivia's mouth with his own to swallow her cries of pleasure.

"How was yours?" he asked, pushing the erotic memory to the back of his mind.

"It was great," Greg said. "Easton, Hudson and Colton are great. We really enjoyed spending the holiday with them."

"I'm sure they had a good time, too," Adam said magnanimously.

"They did," the other man confirmed. "Which makes me wonder why you haven't let Rebecca spend more time with them in the past."

"Is that what she told you?" It was an effort to keep his tone even when his hackles had instinctively risen in response to the other man's remark.

"Are you denying it's true?" Greg challenged.

"Let's just say that my recollection of events is different," Adam decided. "But, for what it's worth, I'm happy for the boys to spend time with Rebecca—and you. Not just on holidays and special occasions, but on a regular schedule through the year."

"I'm glad to hear it."

* * *

"Am I interrupting the great Gilmore baking marathon?"

Olivia felt an immediate tingle when she recognized Adam's voice on the phone. "The last batch of snickerdoodles just went in the oven."

"Does that mean you're free tonight?"

Yes! Anytime. Anywhere.

"As a matter of fact, I am," she said, pleased that she was able to respond calmly, as if her heart wasn't doing a happy dance inside her chest.

"Because the boys and I were thinking of heading into town to see a movie and I was hoping you might want to join us."

Another woman might have been disappointed that he hadn't called to make plans for just the two of them. But Olivia knew that Easton, Hudson and Colton were Adam's world, and she was touched that he would want to include her in their plans.

"What movie is it?"

"Lightyear."

"Ooh, Captain America as a space ranger—I've been looking forward to seeing that one," she said. And waiting a long time for it to finally arrive at the local second-run theater.

"Is that a *yes*?" he asked.

"That depends," she said, not wanting him to know that she was a complete pushover.

"On what?"

"Are you looking for a babysitter or are you asking me on a date?"

He hesitated for just a beat. "I guess I'm asking you on a date."

"You *guess*?"

He huffed out a breath. "I'm asking you on a date, Olivia—albeit with three pint-size chaperones."

"In that case, I accept your invitation."

"Good," he said. "Because it was your idea that we should have at least a couple of dates before we got married."

It was the second time he'd brought up the topic of marriage after dismissing her proposal. Was it possible that he'd changed his mind?

She walked down the hall, out of earshot of her mother, before she responded, "Are you actually considering my proposal?"

"Desperate times call for desperate measures."

"Well, that's flattering," she said dryly.

"I didn't mean that a man would have to be desperate to want to marry you," he was quick to clarify.

"Then please, tell me what you did mean."

"That although I'm still personally opposed to the prospect of marriage, I'm also desperate to hold on to my kids."

"When we talked yesterday, you didn't seem to think that would be a problem. What's changed?"

"I went to bed last night knowing that my boys weren't asleep in their rooms across the hall. And it threw me for a loop, even though I knew that they'd be home today. But then I found myself considering how different everything would be if they lived with Rebecca and only visited me.

"And it occurred to me that Jamie might be right," he

confided now. "That marriage might be the one thing that could make a difference if we get a judge who thinks that a home environment with two parents is preferable to one."

"The always fun *what-if* game," she mused.

"So if you're still open to the prospect of marriage, I think it's something that we should discuss."

It wasn't a very romantic proposal.

In fact, it wasn't a proposal at all.

But Olivia's heart was dancing when she returned to the kitchen to take the last batch of cookies out of the oven.

"Look, Dad! It's Miss Gilmore." Hudson began waving both his arms. "Hi, Miss Gilmore."

Olivia smiled as she walked over to them. "Hello, Morgan family."

"Hey," Easton said.

Colton smiled shyly.

"Miss Gilmore," Adam said.

Though his tone was formal, his gaze was warm—almost intimate—and it heated everything inside Olivia.

She shifted her attention to the buckets of popcorn, tray of drinks and other candy the boys were carrying. "Did you guys leave any snacks at the concession stand for anyone else?"

Colton nodded solemnly. "We dinna get wed vines."

"Not a fan of licorice?" she guessed.

The little boy shook his head.

"We're going to see *Lightyear*," Hudson told her.

"Me, too," she said.

"Really?" His eyes grew wide. "But…it's a kids' movie."

"I disagree," she said. "Pixar movies are for everyone."

"I wanted to see *Jurassic World Dominion*, but Dad said *no* because Colton's too young," Easton told her.

"I said no because you're all too young," Adam said. "The movie's rated PG-13."

"The PG means parental guidance," Easton explained. "And since you're our *parent*, you could *guide* us in watching it."

"Nice try," his dad acknowledged. "But the answer's still no."

"Bennett's dad took him to see it."

"When have you ever known me to be swayed by the fact that Bennett's dad let him do something?"

Easton sighed. "Never."

"So why would you expect that to change now?"

His eldest son didn't bother to respond to the obviously rhetorical question.

"Do you wanna sit with us, Miss Gilmore?" Hudson asked.

"I'd be happy to join you," she said.

So they made their way into the theater together, the boys racing ahead to pick out seats near the back. Colton and Hudson both announced that they wanted to sit by Miss Gilmore. Adam suspected that might have been Easton's preference, too, but his oldest son was too cool to admit it. So Easton sat on the end, with Adam beside him, then Colton, Olivia and Hudson.

It wasn't quite how he'd envisioned a date with Olivia, but if she was seriously considering marrying him, then she needed to understand that his boys were and always would be his priority. And to her credit, if she was at all disappointed by the arrangement, she gave absolutely no indication of it.

"Daddy, I gots to pee!" Colton announced, just as the lights dimmed and the Coming Attractions logo filled the screen.

Adam exhaled a weary sigh. "Of course you do."

"I gots to go *now*!"

"Do you mind staying here with Hudson and Easton?" Adam asked, leaning over Colton's head to whisper in Olivia's ear.

He breathed in the scent of her perfume—the same perfume she'd been wearing last night, when he'd been buried deep inside her, and felt his body stir.

"I'm not going anywhere," she promised, with a wink. "I don't want to miss the coming attractions."

By the time Adam and Colton returned from their visit to the restroom, the lights had completely dimmed. But earlier Olivia had recognized several families that she knew from school and found herself wondering if it had been a mistake to accept Adam's invitation. If her presence here with his family made a statement about their relationship that she wasn't ready to make.

On the other hand, if the prospect of a future wedding was on the table, it would be less of a shock to the community if they'd actually been seen in public together before exchanging vows.

About halfway through the movie, Colton's eyes started to grow heavy. Olivia found herself smiling as she watched his lids start to droop, only for Colton to realize what was happening and open them wide again, fighting valiantly against sleep.

Obviously Adam noticed, too, because she heard him whisper to his youngest son, "You sleepy, buddy?"

Colton shook his head, even as he popped his thumb into his mouth, something she'd learned that he did when he was really tired. Then he shifted in his seat, moving closer to Olivia to rest his head on her shoulder.

"I cuddow wif Miz Gi'mow." He tipped his head back to look at her with those beautiful moss green eyes. "'Kay, Miz Gi'mow?"

She nodded as Colton's thumb crept up to his mouth again, her heart swelling so much that her chest felt tight.

She tried to focus on the screen, but the image was blurry. And though she eventually managed to blink away the tears that filled her eyes, she couldn't shake the conviction that this was what had been missing from her life—a child to snuggle, to nurture, to love.

And that maybe this little boy and his brothers needed her as much as she needed them.

The movie did not disappoint, and Easton and Hudson were chattering happily about their favorite parts as they joined the throng of people exiting the theater. Colton had managed to stay awake through the movie, but as Adam carried him out, his eyes were starting to drift shut again.

"Let me just get the boys buckled in and then I'll walk you to your car," he said to Olivia.

"I can make my own way to my car," she assured

him. "It's more important that you get the boys home and into bed."

"But it doesn't count as a date if I don't get to kiss you good-night."

"Then I guess we'll have to go out again another time."

"Or…" He paused, apparently in an effort to come up with an alternative plan. "I could get them settled into bed at home and come back into town to meet you for a drink later," he finally said. "Maybe at Diggers'?"

"Or… I could come out to the ranch and have a drink with you there," she suggested.

"You wouldn't mind?"

"I think we'll have more privacy there. To talk," she said firmly.

He'd never thought that he'd even consider getting married again, but the prospect of marrying Olivia didn't make him want to run for the hills. Maybe it was because the memory of their lovemaking was still vivid in his mind, but he suspected it was more than just sex. He sincerely enjoyed spending time with her, and it was apparent that the boys were already wild about her—a realization that might have given him pause if it wasn't obvious equally obvious that she was wild about them, too.

His only hesitation was caused by the knowledge of what she would be sacrificing—the chance to fall in love and be loved as she deserved. Because he wasn't going to fall in love with her, and he didn't want her to hold out hope otherwise.

But so long as she was prepared to accept the limits of what he could and couldn't give her, he thought a marriage between them could work. And the prospect of having Olivia in his bed—all night, every night—certainly tipped the balance in favor of marriage.

So much so that he was smiling all the way home—until he got close enough to the ranch to see the flashing lights of the fire trucks in his driveway.

Chapter Fourteen

"What's going on?" Easton asked, leaning forward to peer through the front windshield.

"Is there a fire?" Hudson asked.

Please, God, no.

"I hope not," Adam said, trying to stay calm so that the boys would stay calm.

But inside, he was freaking out a little. He might have been freaking out more, but he didn't see any smoke or flames, which he hoped was a good sign.

"But there's fire trucks," Hudson said.

"Maybe Gramma fell and couldn't get up—like in the commercial," Easton suggested.

"She would have called an ambulance, not the fire department, doofus."

"Don't call your brother names." Adam's response was automatic, his attention focused on the house.

"Maybe she called 911," Hudson said now. "When you call 911, they send police and ambulance and fire trucks. Miss Gilmore told us about 911 at school."

"I know," Easton said, the older and, therefore, more knowledgeable brother. "Miss Gilmore told us about it when I was in her class—*two years ago*."

Adam shifted the vehicle into Park and unfastened his seat belt. "Please stop bickering so you don't wake Colton—and stay right here."

"Where are you going?" Hudson asked.

"Why can't we come with you?" Easton wanted to know.

"Because I need you to stay where I know you're safe while I find out what's going on."

"I know how to use a fire extinguisher," Easton said.

"Do you know how to stay put when I tell you to stay put?" Adam asked, starting to lose patience with the incessant questions.

Easton and Hudson nodded, shrinking a bit at their dad's unusually sharp tone.

"Good. I'll be back as soon as I can, and I expect to find everyone right here when I do. Understood?"

After they nodded again, he closed the car door— quietly so as not to wake Colton—and sprinted toward the house.

The excited anticipation that had fluttered in Olivia's belly when Adam invited her back to his house was supplanted by apprehension when she spotted the fire trucks in his driveway. She leaped out of her vehicle and hurried toward the house, making a sharp detour when she noticed that the windows of Adam's SUV were fogged up.

She tapped on the glass to alert the boys to her presence before she opened the door and kept her voice light as she asked, "What's going on, boys?"

"There's fire trucks at our house!" Hudson said, just a hint of fear underlying the excitement in his voice.

"I can see that."

"Dad told us to stay here until he knew what was going on," Easton confided.

"That sounds like good advice," Olivia said. "Mind if I wait here with you?"

"Nuh-uh," Hudson said.

She settled into the seat, twisting her body around so that she was facing them.

Colton, she noted, was sound asleep in his booster, completely oblivious to all the excitement.

"Why are you at our house?" Easton suddenly asked.

"Your dad invited me to come over so that we could talk about some things."

"Uh-oh," Hudson said. "Whenever Dad says we hafta talk, it usually means we're in trouble."

"Your dad isn't in trouble," she assured them, pulling out her phone to send Adam a quick text message to let him know that she was with the boys.

"Maybe *you're* the one in trouble," Easton said.

"Nobody's in trouble." She started to tuck her phone away again when it chimed to indicate receipt of a message.

All clear. You can bring the boys inside.

"Okay, boys. Your dad says we can go in."

Immediately the back doors opened and Easton and Hudson tumbled out of the vehicle.

"Wait," she said.

They immediately pulled up.

Colton didn't stir, so she got out of the vehicle, too, and reached across the back seat to unbuckle the sleeping child. She staggered a little under his weight as she lifted him into her arms. She had a lot of friends and family members with babies, but she obviously hadn't considered that a five-year-old weighed a lot more than a five-month-old—the age of her cousin Marissa's baby.

"Your dad might still be busy talking to the firefighters," she said to Easton and Hudson, "so he'd probably appreciate it if you went to your rooms and started getting ready for bed. Can you do that?"

They responded with nods, then took off toward the house again.

She followed them through the back door, where they shrugged out of their coats and kicked off their boots before heading up the stairs to the second floor.

"This is mine and Colton's room," Hudson said, pausing at the first door at the top of the stairs and hitting the switch on the wall to illuminate the room. "Easton has his own room, at the end of the hall, but ours is bigger."

"This is a big room," she noted.

It was well laid out, too, so that although the boys had to share the space, they each had clearly defined areas that were their own, complete with a single bed, nightstand and dresser.

She carefully laid Colton on top of the bed with the painted letter *C* affixed to the wall above the headboard.

His pajamas were neatly folded on top of his pillow, and she considered trying to wrangle the little boy out of his clothes and into his pj's without waking him. Then she remembered the candy and popcorn and juice he'd consumed at the movie theater, and she knew there was no way she could let him skip brushing his teeth tonight.

Since waking him was inevitable, she gave him a gentle shake now.

"S'eepy," Colton protested.

"I know," she said. "And as soon as you get your jammies on and your teeth brushed, you can go back to sleep."

With a weary sigh, Colton dragged himself up into a seated position on the bed.

She managed to get the sleepy boy out of his clothes and into his pj's, then carried him to the bathroom to brush his teeth before carrying him back to his bed and tucking him in.

"Kiss," he murmured sleepily.

She leaned down and touched her lips to his cheek. "Sweet dreams."

Hudson climbed into his bed and turned on the light clipped to his headboard. "Dad lets me read for half an hour before bed," he told her.

She glanced at her watch. "It's after nine o'clock already."

"But it's not a school night."

"Why don't we compromise and say you can read until nine thirty? That gives you twenty minutes."

"Okay," he agreed, already opening the cover to the page that had been marked with a Dog Man bookmark.

She walked farther down the door and tapped on Easton's open door.

He had his pajamas on but was on top of the covers on his bed, a book—*The Lightning Thief*—in hand. There was also a graphic novel on his nightstand, but he was obviously ready to transition from the exploits of Captain Underpants to the adventures of a Greek demigod, and it made her heart happy to see the progress he'd made in the two years that had passed since he was in her class.

Like many boys in second grade, he'd struggled with his reading. And though Olivia had tried to reassure Adam that it wasn't an uncommon problem, he'd been worried about his son falling behind. When he'd asked about resources for remedial help, she'd offered to spend extra time with Easton before or after school. So twice a week, on Tuesdays and Thursdays, Easton had spent thirty minutes with her before school. After only a few weeks, the pieces he'd struggled with had clicked together in his brain, and by the end of second grade, he'd been reading above grade level.

"Twenty minutes of reading and then lights out, okay, Easton?"

"Okay," he agreed, not looking up from his book.

By the time she made her way back downstairs, the firefighters had gone, leaving Adam alone in the kitchen with the acrid scent of burned plastic.

"Everything okay?" she asked him.

"Yeah. Mom accidentally put the electric kettle on the stove, melting the plastic on the bottom which set off the smoke detector which led her to call the fire department."

He scrubbed his hands over his face. "I'm going to need a new kettle, but other than that, no real harm was done."

"Your mom's okay?"

"Yeah. Just a little shaken up."

"I imagine you're a little shaken up, too," she said.

"Yeah." He let out a weary sigh. "This was definitely *not* how I envisioned my night ending." And then, as if only now realizing that the house was quiet, he asked, "What are the boys up to? I saw them come in, but they went straight upstairs."

"They're in bed with their pj's on and teeth brushed."

"You got the boys into bed?"

"You seemed to have your hands full with other things, and I had a general idea of their bedtime routines after the weekend in Vegas, so I thought it was something I could help with."

"It was a huge help," he said, sincerely grateful and more than a little stunned. "Thank you."

"Never a dull moment at the Morgan house, huh?"

"Dull moments are my greatest fantasy."

"I think you need to ramp up your fantasies," she told him.

He managed a smile then. "Maybe I should have said that dull moments *were* my greatest fantasy, because after last night, I've found myself dreaming about a sexy teacher in a tack room."

"After last night, I've found myself dreaming about a sexy cowboy in a bed."

He chuckled at that as he made his way to the refrigerator. "Yeah. I bet we could have a lot of fun in a bed." He opened the door and pulled out a bottle of beer, holding it up for her inspection. "Do you want one? Or there's a partial bottle of chardonnay in here, if you'd rather have a glass of wine."

"Would you mind if I made a cup of tea instead?" she asked.

"I wouldn't mind," he said. "But you're going to have some trouble making tea without a kettle."

"All I need is a mug, some water and the microwave. And a tea bag."

He retrieved a mug from the cupboard and handed it to her.

She filled it from the tap, then set it in the microwave and programmed the time.

He opened the cupboard above the stove and read the names on the boxes stacked inside. "We've got black tea, white tea, green tea, Earl Grey, lemon ginger, mandarin-orange spice and peppermint."

"Lemon ginger sounds good," she said.

He wiggled that one out of the pile—and sent an avalanche of boxes tumbling down.

Adam swore; Olivia laughed—then immediately clapped a hand over her mouth.

"I'm sorry," she said. "I know I shouldn't be laughing, but it was kind of funny."

"Don't apologize."

He pulled her hand away from her face, so he could see the smile she was trying to hide, and found his own lips curving. There was just something about her joy that was infectious, allowing him to forget about everything that had gone wrong and focus on what was right—and the woman standing in front of him was at the top of that list.

"I like seeing you smile," he told her. "Even if it's at my expense."

"It's just been one of those days, hasn't it?"

"So it would seem," he agreed.

"I'm still here," she pointed out.

"I can see that."

"I'm just saying—if this is an example of the *worse* part of *for better or for worse*—I'm going to stick. You don't have to worry about that."

"I'm not worried about that." He lifted his beer to his lips and took a long swallow.

"But you're worried about something more than custody of your kids," she guessed, dropping a tea bag into the mug that she'd removed from the microwave.

"Mostly I'm worried that you don't really know what you're getting into."

"So tell me."

"Well, for starters, my mother lives with me."

"I'm aware of that."

"She's been a huge help to me, taking care of the house and the boys. But it's likely that she's going to need more help than she can give in the coming years."

"I understand," she said. "I worry about my parents getting older, too."

"It's more than that," he confided. "She's been a little…absent-minded lately. And I'm not just saying that because she destroyed a kettle tonight."

"Are you referring to the incident at The Trading Post when the cashier had all of her groceries scanned and bagged before your mom realized that she didn't have her wallet?"

He scowled. "How did you hear about that?"

"I was in the next checkout."

"You're the *nice young lady* who paid for her groceries," he realized.

She nodded.

And they both knew that was more significant than the forgotten wallet—because everyone misplaced personal items now and again. But the fact that his mom had forgotten Olivia's name—the woman who'd been her own daughter's best friend since kindergarten—was indicative of a bigger problem.

"I'll pay you back for the groceries," he promised.

"Your mom already did."

He frowned. "When?"

"She came to the school the next day with her checkbook."

"Well, that's something, anyway," he said. "But how many other people were in the store? How many people are whispering that Shirley Morgan is going senile? And how long is it going to take those whispers to reach Rebecca's ears?

"Probably not long," he said, answering his own question. "Because one of the firefighters who was here was a guy I knew from high school, and his older brother is Rebecca's new lawyer. And you know she'll find any reason she can to try to take the boys away from me."

"It doesn't matter how many reasons—real or imagined—she has," Olivia said. "She's the one who chose to walk out on her family, and I can't imagine a judge would change your mutually agreed upon custody arrangement simply because your ex-wife has suddenly decided that she wants more time with the boys."

"I wouldn't think so, either, but now she's claiming that she had diminished capacity when she signed those papers."

"Diminished how?"

"According to the letter her new lawyer sent to my lawyer, she was suffering from postpartum depression."

"Do you think it's true?"

"It would explain some things," he confided. "I know she struggled a little after Easton was born. But having a baby was a big adjustment—for both of us. And she struggled a little more with Hudson. Then, when Colton was born…it was almost as if she completely checked out. And I felt like it was my fault."

"Why would it have been your fault?"

"Because I knew she was hoping for a girl. And I knew that our chance of having a girl, after two boys, was pretty slim."

"Even if it's true—and I'm not in any way diminishing the impact of postpartum depression—she hasn't made any effort to have a real relationship with the boys in more than four years. How's she going to explain that to a judge?"

"I don't know, so I'm trying to focus on doing everything I can to convince the judge that the boys are better off staying with me."

"That's why you want to get married."

"Yeah." But Adam looked troubled rather than reassured.

"What else have you got?" she said. "Because so far, nothing you've said has convinced me that a marriage between us couldn't work."

"You also need to know that I'm not going to fall in love with you," he said.

That arrow hit the mark—slicing straight through her heart.

"Because you're still in love with your ex-wife?" she guessed.

"I told you in Las Vegas that I'm not," he said. "To be honest, I'm not sure I was ever really in love with her."

"So why did you marry her?"

"We got married in October and Easton was born in April—and he wasn't a preemie."

Even most of her second-grade students could count the number of months and know that it was less than nine.

"And then you went on to have two more children together," she pointed out.

"Yeah. We were trying to do the right thing. Trying to make our marriage work. And obviously there were some areas in which we weren't completely incompatible, but aside from decent physical chemistry, we didn't have a lot in common."

"Then why are you so certain you won't fall in love with me?" she asked lightly.

"Because everything I have, I give to my boys," he told her, completely serious. "I don't have anything left for anyone else. So if you still want to get married, I need to know that you understand that, because I don't want to hurt you."

She took a minute to consider his words, acknowledge the warning, before responding. "I understand."

Because she did understand that he was convinced of every word that he was saying. And she thought it was sad, but she didn't believe it was really true.

Because Olivia knew that love didn't follow any kind

of rules, and that it was too big to be put in any kind of box, as he was obviously trying to do.

"And I need to know that you won't fall in love with me, either," he said now.

"I'm not sure that's a promise anyone can make," she told him. "But I can at least assure you that I'm going into this with my eyes wide open."

Still, he looked worried. "I know you'd hoped to meet a terrific guy, fall in love and get married."

She shrugged. "That's the fairy tale, isn't it?"

"And I'm asking you to settle for so much less than you deserve."

"Except that I don't feel as if marrying you would be settling, Adam. In fact, if we decide to go through with this, I'd feel incredibly lucky. Because the truth is, I never wanted the fairy-tale prince so much as I wanted a family."

"So now we're getting to the real reason you want to marry me—to be a mother?"

"That's one of the reasons," she agreed. "The other is the promise of a lot more phenomenal sex."

"That definitely weighs heavily in favor on my scales," he told her. "But what's going to happen if we get married and then you meet that terrific guy?"

She wasn't worried about that possibility, because she knew that she already had—and he was the guy. The only man she'd ever loved. The only one she'd ever dreamed of marrying.

But there was no way she could say any of that to Adam—not if she wanted him to go through with this plan.

"If it hasn't happened in the past ten years, I don't

imagine it's going to happen in the next ten," she said lightly.

"So you're saying I can count on you to stick around for at least the next decade?"

"If we exchange vows, you'll be stuck with me forever," she told him.

"Thanks for the warning."

"It's not a warning, it's a promise." She took her empty mug to the sink. "And now I really have to go. It's late and your mornings start early."

"They do," he agreed, walking with her to the door.

"Thank you for inviting me to the movie tonight—and sharing your popcorn."

"Thank you for being the calm in the eye of the storm."

"I was happy to help." She reached for the door handle, but he caught her hand and turned her around again.

"It's not a date if it doesn't end with a kiss," he said, right before his lips covered hers.

"I guess it was a date," she acknowledged, when he finally eased away from her.

"And right now, I'm really wishing that you didn't have to go. I'm also wishing that my mother wasn't asleep down the hall and my three kids in their beds upstairs."

"Me, too," she admitted.

"Of course, none of them are light sleepers, so—"

"Good night, Adam."

"Good night, Olivia. Text me when you get home."

"You're dead on your feet," she pointed out gently. "I don't want you waiting up another half an hour for a text message."

"I won't sleep until I hear from you," he assured her.

She didn't doubt it was true. Adam was that type of guy—and it was only one of the reasons she loved him.

But she would keep her word—and keep the true depth of her feelings to herself.

"I'll text you when I get home," she promised.

Chapter Fifteen

Olivia had been teaching long enough to know that when her students returned to class after the Thanksgiving weekend, they were likely to be a little unfocused, already looking forward to Christmas. On Tuesday, they had another reason to be distracted.

It was snowing.

And there was a whole wall of windows on one side of her classroom through which they could all see the big, fluffy white flakes swirling in the sky.

Snow in the desert wasn't so common that her seven- and eight-year-old students were immune to its magical beauty. Truth be told, she wasn't immune to it, either, and it was an effort to tear her gaze away from the windows to the clock on the wall at the back of her classroom.

At recess, they couldn't get outside fast enough—

excited to make snowmen or snow forts or snow angels. Their excitement was infectious, and Olivia was admittedly a little disappointed that she wasn't on duty, so she had no excuse to go outside with them. Instead, she tweaked her next lesson in the hope that they might actually learn something today.

"Welcome back, class," she said, as they returned to their desks, their cheeks flushed with excitement as much as cold.

"Why are there papers on our desks?" Scotty asked suspiciously.

"Because today I'm going to introduce you to the pop quiz."

There were some groans from those students who immediately recognized that *quiz* was another word for *test*.

"But you didn't tell us to study anything," Peyton protested.

"That's because a pop quiz is a surprise test."

Clive had his head down and was already writing on his page.

"What are you doing, Clive?"

"I know how to spell all of this week's vocabulary words," he said.

"This isn't a spelling test," she told him.

"But first period after recess on Tuesday is language."

"You're right," she confirmed. "And today we're going to learn about homonyms."

His eyebrows drew together. "I don't know how to spell that."

She took the paper he'd already started writing on and turned it over so that he had a clean page. "Anyone who needs to sharpen their pencils, please do so now."

She walked down the center aisle and handed a sharpened pencil to Elysia. She was a good student, always attentive in class and willing to help others who needed it, but she never seemed to have a pencil on hand.

The girl's cheeks flushed as she accepted the proffered writing instrument. "Thank you, Miss Gilmore."

"You're welcome." Olivia shifted her attention to survey the class and confirm that everyone was ready. "Now who remembers the first thing you should always do when you're given a test paper?"

A dozen hands immediately shot up into the air. "Charlie," she said, choosing one of the students who didn't always volunteer a response.

"Put your name on it."

"That's right," she confirmed. "So let's start with that."

Nineteen heads dutifully bent over their desks.

"And remember to print legibly so that I can read it."

She waited until all of her students had completed the task, not at all surprised that Ana finished much more quickly than Evangeline.

"Now I'm going to ask you some questions about soda pop. Number one…"

Adam had always believed that his life wasn't just busy but full, leaving him with neither the time nor the inclination for a romantic relationship. All that had changed after the first kiss he'd shared with Olivia. And changed some more after Thanksgiving. Since then, he'd exchanged text messages with her at least a couple of times during the day and talked to her later at night, after the boys were tucked into their beds.

He liked hearing her voice before he went to sleep, though he would have much preferred to have her sleeping beside him.

"How was your day?" he asked, when she connected the call.

"Hectic," she said. "As much as I love teaching, there are some days when it's just really hard to keep the kids focused—and most of those days are in December."

"I heard something about a pop quiz about soda pop."

"We were learning about homonyms today," Olivia explained.

"And if my second-grade teacher had been as creative as you, I might know what that word means."

She chuckled. "Homonyms are words that are spelled the same but have different meanings. Like *pop*—which can refer to soda or the sound of something inflated with air breaking or, in reference to a test, spontaneous."

"Well, Hudson thought it was pretty cool that he got one hundred percent on a test he didn't even study for."

"I'll let you in on a secret," she said. "There were no wrong answers. Everyone who wrote something down in response to each of the questions got full marks.

"But actually, Hudson got one hundred and ten percent, because he earned bonus marks for one of his answers being a homonym."

"Let me guess—orange."

"See, you do know something about homonyms," she said. "Of course, Hudson wasn't the only student who said that orange was his favorite soda flavor, but only Hudson and Clive knew that the word referred to not only the flavor and color but also the fruit itself from which both are derived."

"Now I'm even more grateful their grandparents started college funds for the boys," he remarked.

"Well, you do have a few more years before they'll be packing their bags for UNLV," Olivia said, laughing. "But it's because kids spend so much time in school that I try to make learning fun for everyone in my class."

"From the discussions I've overheard in my kitchen, you're succeeding," he told her.

"I'm happy to hear that," she said. "Now tell me what's new at Morgan's Glen."

"Nothing's new," he said. "But Rebecca called today to confirm that she wants the boys this weekend."

"So much for your theory that she'd grow bored of playing mom."

"Yeah," he agreed. "Which got me thinking that maybe we should set a date for our wedding."

"I'm free after school tomorrow," she said. "We could pop over to town hall then."

He chuckled again. "How about Friday? The boys will still be home Friday, and that gives us time to catch our respective families up on our plans."

"Friday sounds good," she agreed, wondering how she'd let herself get so caught up in the excitement of marrying Adam that she'd forgotten about everyone and everything else.

"Don't forget to pack a bag," he said. "Because there's no way I'm sleeping alone on my wedding night."

"I'll pack a bag," she promised.

"I noticed that you've been spending a lot of time with Olivia Gilmore lately," his mom remarked, when he returned to the house for breakfast after seeing the boys off to school Wednesday morning.

Deciding that there would never be a more perfect segue, Adam said, "I have. And, in fact, we're going to get married."

"Married," she echoed, frowning a little as she scooped eggs onto a plate. "Well, that's a little…unexpected."

"You don't sound happy," he noted, filling a mug with coffee from the pot on the warmer. "I thought you'd be happy."

A few slices of bacon and two pieces of toast joined the eggs. "Are *you* happy?"

"I'm happy," he said, and smiled to prove it.

"Then I'm happy for you." She set his plate on the table. "And I'll call Jack Green tomorrow to see if he knows of any suitable apartments available for rent."

"Jack Green retired several years ago," he reminded his mom.

"I meant JJ," she said, referring to "Jack Junior"—the retired real estate agent's son. "I'll call JJ tomorrow."

"There's no need to call JJ," Adam said. "Unless you're suddenly unhappy with your living arrangements here."

"You know I'm not, but your bride might not want her husband's mother living under the same roof."

"Olivia loves you almost as much as I do."

"She loves me because I'm Jamie's mom," Shirley acknowledged. "She might feel different when I'm her mother-in-law."

"You're right," he noted. "She might love you even more."

Shirley managed a smile then as she began to spread

peanut butter on a slice of toast. "Have you set a date for the wedding? Spring is a popular time for weddings, though it doesn't give you a lot of time to plan. But autumn's lovely, too. Of course, Olivia might prefer summer, when she's not teaching, but don't forget that Jamie and Thomas have already claimed the first Saturday in August."

"Actually, we have set a date," he said, responding to her initial question. "Friday."

"What Friday?"

"*This* Friday."

"You can't possibly plan a wedding in two days," she protested.

"We don't want a big wedding—we just want to be married."

"Are those your words or hers?"

"Both."

"Because most women dream about their wedding day long before they've met the man they're going to marry, and I don't know anyone who ever dreamed of a quick ceremony at town hall."

Adam refused to let his mother's comments dissuade him from his plans—the next step of which was to tell his sons about the upcoming nuptials.

He didn't think they'd have any objections. They certainly hadn't been fazed by Rebecca's marriage. But they didn't live with Rebecca, and part of the reason—the biggest part—he was doing this was to ensure that they could stay at Morgan's Glen.

But while their living arrangements would remain unaltered, marrying Olivia would inevitably change other things, and he needed to be sure that his boys were onboard with the plan. He'd invited Olivia to be there with him to share the news, but she'd suggested that he should do so on his own, so that their reactions wouldn't be tempered by her presence.

He perched on the edge of the tub to supervise their toothbrushing, and after they'd finished spitting and rinsing, he said, "I want to talk to you about something."

"Uh-oh," Hudson said.

"Why do you think it's an uh-oh?"

"Because the last time you wanted to talk, you told us that mom was getting married," Easton said.

"And that wasn't so bad, was it?"

Hudson shrugged. "I liked Las Vegas."

"I wiked the cake," Colton said.

Easton remained silent, wary.

"And your new stepdad seems like a decent guy," Adam said, in an effort to move the conversation forward.

"I guess he's alright," Hudson agreed.

"Well, I've decided that it's time for me to get married again, so you'll have a stepmom, too."

"We don't need a stepmom," Hudson immediately protested. "Stepmothers are evil."

"Why would you say that?" Adam asked.

"Haven't you read *Cinderella*?" Hudson challenged.

"And Cinderella's stepmom only made her clean the castle," Easton chimed in. "Snow White's tried to poison her."

Colton's lower lip quivered. "I don' wanna stepmom."

Adam lifted the little guy onto his knee as he shot a pointed look at the boy's older brothers.

"Cinderella and Snow White are characters in storybooks," he explained. "They're not real. And I promise you, Olivia won't be an evil stepmom."

"Wait a minute," Easton said, holding up a hand. "Are you going to marry *Miss Gilmore*?"

"I am," he confirmed.

The boys' worried expressions immediately and simultaneously transformed, scowls and frowns giving way to smiles.

"So, do you still think you don't need a stepmom?" he asked them.

"We don't *need* one," Hudson insisted. "But I think Miss Gilmore would be okay."

"I wike Miz Gi-mow," Colton said.

"I'm happy to hear that," Adam said. "Easton—are you going to say anything else?"

His eldest son lifted a shoulder. "It's cool."

"When's the wedding?" Hudson's demand was immediately followed by another question. "And do I hafta wear a tie again?"

"We were thinking that we'd go to town hall to get married, so no, you wouldn't have to wear a tie."

"What's town haw?" Colton asked.

"It's where the people in charge of the town work," Adam explained to his youngest son.

"Is Miz Gi-mow gonna weah a fancy dwess?"

"I don't think so."

He should have been prepared for the questions. After Rebecca's nuptials, of course, they would expect something similar.

"Some people have big fancy weddings, some people

have smaller, simpler gatherings and some people go to town hall to exchange their vows in front of a judge."

And having done the big wedding thing once already—Adam didn't see any need to do it all again.

Which, thanks to his mom, he realized now, was a remarkably self-centered approach to the whole thing. Because Olivia had never been married before, and if she'd meant what she'd said about this being a real, forever marriage, it was her only chance for a real wedding.

But she hadn't given any indication that she wanted all the bells and whistles. In fact, she was the one who'd suggested a civil ceremony at town hall, even if he knew the suggestion had been made in consideration of what was expedient and wasn't necessarily a reflection of what she wanted. And in light of how much she was already giving up to help him out, was it fair to ask her to give up her dream of a proper wedding, too?

Adam didn't think so.

Olivia had decided to tell her parents about her wedding plans at their weekly Wednesday night dinner, but when she arrived at the Circle G, she noticed that there were only two places set at the table.

"Dad's not eating with us?"

"He went into Elko with Uncle David today to look at a new baler, and they decided to grab dinner there."

"Oh."

"I didn't think you'd mind if it was just the two of us," Angela said.

"Of course I don't mind," Olivia told her. "I just have some news that I wanted to share with both of you."

"What's the news?"

She didn't know why she was so nervous. She was sure her mom would be happy for her. Well, reasonably sure, anyway.

"Adam and I are getting married."

The whisk that Angela had picked up to stir the gravy slipped out of her hand, bounced off the edge of the counter and fell to the floor. "You're *engaged*?"

Olivia nodded and bent to retrieve the utensil, carrying it to the sink to wash it under the tap.

"To Adam Morgan?"

She nodded again.

Angela began slicing through the meat, wielding the sharp knife with more force than was necessary, while her daughter whisked the gravy. "When did this happen?"

"We've been talking about it since Thanksgiving."

Her mother's lips pressed into a thin line. "He didn't ask your father's permission."

"It's the twenty-first century, Mom."

"It's traditional to ask the bride's father for permission."

"Anyway," Olivia said, eager to move on. "The wedding's on Friday."

"Friday—as in two days from now?"

"That's right."

Her mother mumbled under her breath in Italian as she made the sign of the cross. "Are you pregnant?"

She sighed. "No, Mom. I'm not pregnant."

"Then why are you doing this?" Angela demanded. "Why are you rushing into marriage with a man you've never even been on a real date with?"

"I've known Adam for twenty years," she reminded her mom.

"As your best friend's older brother," Angela acknowledged. "Not to mention that, for five of those years, he was married to another woman. In fact, he has three children with that other woman."

"Yes, he does," she agreed. "Three amazing children who desperately need a real mother."

Angela's gaze sharpened. "Is that what this is about?"

Olivia winced at her slip, but only inwardly.

The key to dealing with her mother, she knew from experience, was not to show any sign of weakness.

"It's about the fact that I love Easton, Hudson and Colton as much as I love their dad—and I thought you would be thrilled to have three more grandchildren to spoil."

Angela's expression softened then, and her lips curved a little. "You know I would—and I will. But your dad…" Her words trailed off on a sigh.

Olivia frowned. "You don't think he'll accept Adam's sons as his grandsons?"

Having seen Charles with Elliott and Avenlea, she couldn't imagine it was true. In fact, she'd heard her dad tell Lindsay that family was about love, not blood, and that's why she and her children had been part of the Gilmore family long before Mitchell put a ring on her finger.

"Of course he will," her mom agreed. "But when Mitchell and Lindsay got married…well, he got a little misty-eyed thinking about your wedding, about walking you down the aisle."

Charles Gilmore misty-eyed?

"Oh." Olivia swallowed, feeling a little emotional herself as she pictured the scene she'd imagined so many times—aching at the realization that her plans would deprive both of them of that moment.

But a wedding was only a moment; a marriage was a lifetime.

"You didn't think about that, did you?" Angela asked her now.

Olivia shook her head slowly. "No," she admitted. "And I should have. I'm sorry."

"You're our only daughter, *cara*."

"I know."

"And if what you really want is to marry Adam Morgan, we will, of course, support you. But let us give you a proper wedding."

"Adam's divorced, so we can't get married in the Catholic church," she reminded her mother.

"There are a lot of options between the church and town hall," Angela pointed out.

"And we really don't want to wait. We want to start living our lives together, and we want to set a good example for his children."

"Would a couple of weeks really make such a difference?"

"I guess not," she said, relenting. "But I'm not agreeing to anything until I talk to Adam."

"But you will talk to him about having a proper wedding?"

"You think you can plan a proper wedding in a couple of weeks?"

Angela rolled up her sleeves. "Watch me."

Chapter Sixteen

"This is a surprise," Olivia said, when she looked up from the papers she was marking to see Adam standing in the doorway of her classroom the following afternoon.

"Is it okay that I stopped by?" he asked.

"Of course," she said. "But if you're looking for Hudson, the bus is already gone."

"I know—I was looking for you."

"Any particular reason?"

"I've been thinking about something," he began.

"Sounds like it's something important," she noted.

"I think so."

She closed the folder of papers to give him her full attention.

"After talking to my mom yesterday morning and the boys last night, I don't think we should get married—"

"What?" Olivia's heart dropped out of her chest and went splat on the ground. "Why?"

"You didn't let me finish," he chided gently. "I'm not saying that we shouldn't get married, only that we shouldn't get married at town hall."

"Oh." She exhaled a shaky sigh of relief. "What changed your mind?"

"The boys had all kinds of questions about whether you were going to wear a fancy dress and if there was going to be a big cake, and I know we didn't plan to do any of that, but I don't want them to get the impression that this wedding—this marriage—is any less real than Rebecca and Greg's."

"Except that Rebecca and Greg are in love, and we're not." She felt a pang as she said the words, but forced herself to tamp down the emotion, knowing it wouldn't be the last time she had to do so.

"There was a time when she claimed to love me, too, so I'm not sure those words should carry much weight. On the other hand, you and I are both committed to making our marriage work, which I think gives us better odds of actually succeeding."

"You should be careful about tossing around such romantic declarations," Olivia cautioned lightly. "You're going to make my heart flutter."

She was joking, mostly, but Adam didn't smile.

In fact, his expression grew more serious.

"You deserve romance," he said. "You deserve so much more than what I'm offering you."

"You're offering me everything I've ever wanted," she assured him.

"A husband and a family."

You.

But, of course, she didn't say that. She didn't want him to know that she'd been in love with him for fifteen years. Because he'd been very clear that he wasn't going to fall in love with her, and she suspected that if he knew her heart was already engaged, he'd refuse to follow through with their plan.

I don't want to hurt you, he'd said.

And she knew he meant it.

But she was so completely and irrevocably in love with him that she was willing to accept whatever he was willing to give her. Maybe he wouldn't love her, but she would have a life with him, share his bed, help raise his children. It really was more than she'd ever dreamed of.

"So what did you have in mind for our wedding?" she asked.

"Why don't we discuss it over dinner tonight?"

"That sounds good," she agreed. "I'm got some things to finish up here, but I could meet you at Diggers' in about an hour."

"I don't want to meet you at Diggers'," he said. "I want to pick you up at your door and take you somewhere a little nicer than the local bar and grill."

"Like a real date?" she said teasingly.

"Like a real date," he confirmed, glancing at his watch. "Six o'clock, okay?"

"Sure," she agreed.

He lowered his head and gave her a quick kiss. "I'll see you then."

She waited until he was gone before she gave in to the urge to do a happy dance, excited beyond belief that she had a date with the man she was going to marry.

* * *

The parking lot was located across the street from the restaurant Adam had chosen in Battle Mountain, so he dropped Olivia at the door to wait inside where it was warm while he parked. She'd heard good things about The Chophouse, though she'd never dined there herself. As she waited in the vestibule for her date, the fabulous scent of grilled meat gave her hope that the restaurant would live up to its reputation.

The interior boasted lots of stone, wood and leather, the tables set with slate-blue linen napkins, gleaming silver and sparkling crystal. Flickering tealight candles in shallow glass bowls supplemented the soft overhead lighting and added a subtle hint of romance.

She stepped away from the door when it opened from the other side—and felt her jaw drop when Leo Delissio walked in.

"Olivia." A quick smile spread across his face. "It's so good to see you." He gave her a quick hug before pulling back again to ask, "But what are you doing here?"

"I'm here for dinner."

"Of course," he said, shaking his head. "Me, too. I mean, I'm picking up dinner to refuel before another double shift tonight."

"Obviously you're still keeping busy at the hospital."

"Too busy," he said. "As you well know."

"A good doctor is always going to be in demand," she acknowledged.

The hostess approached, carrying a paper takeout bag. "Your order, Dr. Delissio."

"Thank you."

"My pleasure." She turned her attention to Olivia. "Can I help you with something?"

"Oh. Um. I'm just waiting for…my date," she admitted, feeling inexplicably guilty. Which was ridiculous. After all, it wasn't as if she and Leo had ever agreed to be exclusive, and she hadn't heard from him since their brief telephone conversation the day she'd received his flowers.

"Do you want me to show you to your table while you're waiting?"

"No, thanks. I'll wait here," Olivia said, and the hostess drifted away again.

"So…you're seeing someone," Leo noted.

She nodded.

"Is it serious?"

"We're talking about marriage, so I'd say it's pretty serious."

"Well, I guess the chances of me getting to second base on our next date have just dropped exponentially," he said lightly.

"I'm sorry. I should have—"

He cut her off with a laugh. "You don't need to apologize to me, Olivia. I'm the one who blew my chance with you."

"I do need to apologize," she insisted. "Or at least explain. I wasn't seeing anyone else while we were dating, but I've known Adam for a long time and, recently, things just clicked between us."

"He's a lucky man," Leo said.

"I feel pretty lucky these days, too."

"I'm happy for you."

"Thank you."

"And if you have any friends who are as beautiful and kind and charming as you, and who don't mind being stood up on the rare occasion that an emergency arises—which occasions maybe aren't so rare," he acknowledged wryly, "please feel free to give them my number."

"I'll do that," she promised. "Though I suspect that there are plenty of female doctors or nurses or others who work at the hospital who'd be more than happy to go out on a date with the amazing Dr. Delissio."

"Date someone from the hospital?" He feigned horror at the thought. "Why would I do that? Their hours are insane."

Olivia chuckled softly. "I'm really glad I ran in to you today."

"So am I," he said. "And not only because it saves me the potential embarrassment of your new husband answering your phone the next time I called to ask you out."

It wasn't Adam's first visit to The Chophouse, but it was his first time there for pleasure rather than business. As the hostess led them to the quiet corner in the back of the restaurant that he'd requested, he hoped Olivia would be pleased with his choice of venue for their meal.

"This place is seriously impressive," Olivia said, when the hostess had left them with their menus.

"Wait until you try the food," he told her.

"So you didn't bring me to this out-of-town restaurant because you didn't want to spark gossip by being seen with me in Haven?"

"What would be the point in that when we're undoubtedly going to spark a whole firestorm of gossip when news of our engagement gets out?"

"None," she admitted, as a young server in a black vest and pants approached their table.

After introducing himself as Dale, he filled their water glasses and recited the daily specials before taking their drink orders and disappearing again.

"See anything you like on the menu?" Adam asked.

"Too many things," she confided. "I'm usually pretty decisive, but I'm having a tough time deciding between the beef tenderloin medallions and the filet mignon."

"You get an extra two ounces of meat with the medallions," he said. "So if you're really hungry, I'd go with those."

"I am hungry. But as we made our way to our table, we passed a couple sharing a slice of decadent-looking chocolate cake, so I think I'm going to want to save room for dessert."

"You *definitely* want to save room for dessert," Dale confirmed, as he delivered their drinks to the table. "People come to The Chophouse for the steak, but they stay for our twelve-layer chocolate-mousse cake."

"I'm sold," she said, closing the leather folder of her menu.

"Did you want a starter or main course or just the cake?" the server asked, with a wink.

"I guess I should see if the steak lives up to its reputation," she said. "I'll have the filet mignon, medium, with roasted broccoli."

"Excellent choice," Dale said, before turning his attention to Adam. "And for you, sir?"

"I'm going to try the New York strip, also medium, with the au gratin potatoes."

"Any food allergies or sensitivities?" Dale asked, as he collected their menus.

They both answered in the negative and the server promised to be back with some warm bread and house-churned honey butter.

"Do not let me have bread," Olivia said to Adam.

"Why not?"

"Because I'll fill up on bread and then I won't have room for dessert—and I really want to try that chocolate cake."

He chuckled at that. "Worst-case scenario, you can get a slice of the chocolate cake to take home."

"I'll keep that in mind," she promised. "And while I appreciate you bringing me here, it seems a little out of the way when you can get a really good steak at The Home Station."

"I know, but The Home Station serves Gilmore beef exclusively," he pointed out.

"Which is really good beef." She grinned with pride.

"I wouldn't dare argue with that," he said, appreciating her loyalty to the family brand. "But The Chophouse buys from me."

"How did I not know that?"

"Our partnership is fairly recent."

"Yours and mine—or yours with the restaurant?"

"I was referring to the restaurant, although the statement applies equally to both," he acknowledged.

"Still, if you wanted a Morgan steak, wouldn't it have been easier—and cheaper—to fire up your grill at home?"

"Sure," he agreed. "But it wouldn't have been nearly as romantic, and I wanted to give you at least a little bit of romance."

"I appreciate the effort," she told him. "But it really wasn't necessary. I've already agreed to marry you."

"Even though I haven't yet asked you properly," he noted.

"Considering that our reasons for getting married are hardly traditional, I don't expect a traditional proposal."

"You should always expect the unexpected," he said.

And then he pushed his chair away from the table and dropped to one knee on the floor, holding up an antique diamond-cluster engagement ring.

"Olivia Gilmore—will you marry me?"

She knew his proposal was only a formality, and yet, seeing him on one knee, something inside her quivered. Because a real proposal suddenly made their impending nuptials so much more real.

And because this moment really was her greatest wish come true.

Adam Morgan, the man she'd been in love with since she was fifteen, offering her a ring.

Okay, maybe in her fantasies he was giving her his heart along with the ring, but he'd made it clear that this was the best offer she was going to get, and she didn't hesitate to take it.

"Yes, Adam Morgan, I will marry you."

As the diners around them politely applauded, he took her left hand and slid the ring onto her third finger. Then he rose to his feet to brush his lips over hers. A wolf whistle rang out over the applause.

"We're going to need to get that sized," Adam noted,

when he sat down across from her again. "Your fingers are more slender than Grandma Jeannie's."

"I remember Grandma Jeannie," she said, staring at the sparkling cluster of diamonds on her finger. "This was her ring?"

He nodded. "It came to me when she passed."

Which she knew had been about eight years earlier, because Rebecca had been pregnant with Hudson at the funeral.

"But if you don't like it, or you'd rather have something different—"

"It's perfect. A little big," she acknowledged, curling her fingers into her palm so the ring wouldn't slide off. "But otherwise, perfect."

Dale returned to the table then, with the promised bread and butter and another server bearing an ice bucket with a split of champagne and two flute glasses.

"Compliments of the manager," the other server said, as he deftly uncorked the bottle. "With congratulations on your engagement."

"Thank you," Adam said.

"He must really like your meat," Olivia remarked.

The server gave her an odd look that made her realize how her statement might have been misinterpreted, causing heat to flood her cheeks.

"I didn't mean—he's Adam Morgan," she explained. "Of Morgan Cattle and Beef."

Of course, the server probably didn't know anything about their suppliers and cared even less.

"Ohmygod." She lifted her hands to her heated cheeks when he was gone. "I'm so embarrassed!"

"Don't be," Adam said. "You're really cute when you blush."

"Cute?" she said dubiously.

"Very cute," he assured her. "But you're also smart and sexy and amazingly patient with my kids."

"Well, don't you know how to turn on the charm." She smiled her thanks to Dale—her cheeks still pink—when he delivered their meals. "And now that we're officially engaged, I guess we should set a new date for our wedding."

"How does December twentieth sound?"

"Really far away."

"It's less than three weeks from today," he told her.

"And only five days before Christmas."

"But Eberley Gardens is available on the twentieth."

"What's Eberley Gardens?"

"The new name of Hiram Blum's ranch, which the new owners have turned into an event venue. There's a renovated barn on the property that I thought might be a step up from town hall."

"I love the idea of getting married in an old barn," she admitted. "But I thought, in the interest of keeping things simple, we'd have the ceremony at my parents' house at the Circle G."

"Your parents have a big house," he acknowledged. "But even if we rearranged all the furniture, it doesn't really lend itself to creating an aisle—and your dad wants to walk you down the aisle."

"How do you know what my dad wants?"

He lifted one shoulder. "I might have stopped by the

Circle G this afternoon, on my way into town, to ask his permission to marry you."

And that reluctant confession would have been enough to make Olivia fall head over heels in love—if she wasn't already there.

Chapter Seventeen

Adam was stuck at the ranch Sunday afternoon, waiting for the vet, so he was grateful that Olivia was available to pick up the boys from Rebecca's house. He could have asked his mom, and he knew Shirley wouldn't have balked at the request, but he wasn't entirely comfortable asking her to get behind the wheel of a vehicle these days.

Thankfully Dr. Stafford was able to quickly diagnose and treat the downed animal for a magnesium deficiency, so that by the time Adam sat down to dinner with his family, he was in a much better mood than when Olivia had left to get the boys.

It was just the five of them tonight, as his mom had gone to the Circle G to help Olivia's mom with wedding stuff. He'd been grateful for Olivia's offer to cook, and she'd promised a stir-fry with an orange ginger marinade that would trick his sons into gobbling up their vegetables. So far, it seemed to be working.

Easton, Hudson and Colton were happy to share details about their weekend in between bites of food.

"And then we went to Adventure Village and we played mini putt and video games," Hudson said, stabbing his fork into a baby corn.

Adam was familiar with Adventure Village—a local recreation park that offered various family-friendly activities and was a popular venue for kids' birthday parties.

"We even got to drive the go-karts," Easton said. "Well, I got to drive, because I'm fifty-four inches tall. Hudson had to ride with Savanna and Colton went with Simon."

"Wait a minute." Adam made the time-out signal with his hands. "Who are Savanna and Simon?"

"The babysitter and her boyfriend."

Babysitter?

His ex-wife, who was fighting him for custody of their sons, had hired a babysitter during her weekend visit with them?

"Adam." Olivia touched a hand to his arm. "Let's not jump to any conclusions here, okay?"

He nodded stiffly. "What can you guys tell me about Savanna?"

"She has blue hair," Hudson told him.

"It's pwetty," Colton said.

"How old is she?"

The boys exchanged glances, shrugs.

"Dunno," Hudson said.

"But she's pretty old," Easton added.

"Why do you say that?"

"'Cuz she's in high school and has her driver's license."

High school?

Adam pushed his chair away from the table. "I have to run out for a minute."

Olivia jumped up and followed him to the foyer. "This isn't a good idea, Adam."

"What's not a good idea?"

She glanced back toward the kitchen and lowered her voice. "Confronting Rebecca when you're obviously angry."

"I want to know what the hell she was thinking, letting our children ride in go-karts with a teenage babysitter and her boyfriend."

"I understand you're upset," she began.

"Damn right, I'm upset."

"And you have every reason to be," she agreed. "I just think this is something you should probably discuss with Katelyn instead of rushing off to confront your ex-wife."

"I will," he promised. "But I'm going to discuss it with Rebecca first."

It wasn't until Adam was pounding on the door of his ex-wife's new house on Miners' Pass that he realized Olivia was probably right. That he was reacting emotionally rather than reasonably and that a confrontation with Rebecca wasn't likely to solve anything. That it might actually make the situation worse.

The smart thing would be to turn around and go home.

But a teenage babysitter?

He just couldn't wrap his head around it.

"Adam. What are you doing here?"

His ex-wife was wearing an oversize sweater and rib-knit leggings, her hair in a haphazard knot on top of her head. Her face was pale and there were dark circles under her eyes.

"Are you sick?"

She blinked, obviously startled by the question. "What? No. I'm just…tired."

"Because you look like hell."

"Thank you for noticing."

"Where's Greg?"

"He's out of town on business." She folded her arms over her chest and asked again, "What are you doing here?"

"I wanted to talk to you."

With a sigh, she stepped away from the door, allowing him to enter the foyer.

"Becky, is it okay if— Oh." A blue-haired teenager skidded on the marble floor, a chagrined expression on her face. "Sorry. I didn't realize you had company."

"Adam isn't company—he's my ex-husband," Rebecca said. "Adam, this is Savanna, Greg's niece."

"You're the dad," Savanna said. "Great kids."

"Thanks," he said, automatically shaking her proffered hand.

"What did you need, Savanna?" Rebecca asked.

"I wondered if I could borrow your car to go see Tasha."

"Weren't you just FaceTiming with Tasha?"

"Yeah, but she and Crank broke up, so she needs some face-to-face time."

"You know where the keys are," Rebecca told her.

"Thanks. I won't be late." Then to Adam she said, "It was nice meeting you."

"You, too," he automatically replied.

"Savanna's staying with us for a couple weeks," Rebecca said, as the door closed behind the teen. "She's a good kid. Smart. Responsible. But she butts heads with her mom, so she's bunking here while they work through some things."

"You just called her a kid," he pointed out.

"So?"

"So I want to know what you were thinking letting that *kid* and her boyfriend take our kids to Adventure Village."

"I was thinking that they'd enjoy it—and they did. In fact, they couldn't stop talking about how much fun they had."

"That isn't the point," he said.

"I think it is the point. I think you're mad because they had a good time with me."

"But they didn't," he pointed out. "They had a good time with Savanna and Simon. Did you even spend any time with them over the weekend?"

"Of course I did. And I originally planned to go to Adventure Village with them, but...I just wasn't feeling up to it."

His gaze narrowed. "You said you weren't sick."

"I'm not." Her eyes filled with tears. "I'm pregnant."

Adam had to pick up his jaw from her polished marble floor before he could speak. "But...how?"

She managed a laugh then. "After three kids, I would have expected you to figure out how babies are made."

"What I'm struggling to understand," he clarified, "is how you got pregnant with your tubes tied." Because he knew she'd had the procedure done after giving birth to Colton.

"It turns out that, five years after tubal ligation, thirteen women out of every thousand will become pregnant."

"And you're one of the thirteen."

She sniffed. "Who said thirteen isn't a lucky number?"

"I don't know if I should offer condolences or congratulations," he admitted.

"I didn't want another baby," she said. "I don't even know how to be a good mom to the kids that I've got... but I'm trying."

He knew that she was. He wasn't sure her efforts would last, but certainly she'd been in regular contact with the boys since she and Greg returned from their honeymoon. And he was happy to facilitate the extra visits, but he wasn't happy that she was trying to take his boys away from him—and he still struggled to understand what had prompted her action.

"Why are you really fighting for custody?" he asked her now.

"Because Greg and I both thought he'd given up the possibility of ever having a child of his own when he married me, but if we had custody of Easton, Hudson and Colton, he could at least be a dad to them."

"*Step*dad," Adam said pointedly.

"But now..."

"If you don't want to have the baby..."

He let the words trail off, because it wasn't any of his business. Any decisions about Rebecca's pregnancy should be made by her and her husband. But knowing what she'd gone through with each of her previous pregnancies, he couldn't deny that he was a little concerned.

"I want the baby," she said, sniffling. "I really do. But my boobs are sore and I'm nauseated all the time and…I'm scared."

"What are you afraid of?"

"That I'm going to mess up with this baby like I messed up with ours."

"I don't know why we're here," Jamie said, as she followed her friend into Bliss Boutique Tuesday afternoon. "I thought you said we were going Christmas shopping."

"We're here because I found a dress that I'm thinking of buying for a Christmas event," Olivia told her. "Which technically makes it Christmas shopping."

"That's a stretch."

"I know, but I'm asking you to indulge me, anyway." She steered her friend into a chair. "Sit."

Jamie sat and pulled out her phone to review her shopping list while Olivia ducked into the change room at the back of the designer dress shop.

Astrid, the shop owner who'd been a huge help when Olivia and her mom had visited on Saturday, was already there, waiting to help her into the dress she'd selected.

"I've got a ton of presents still to buy, then wrap," Jamie said, talking to her through the curtain. "Plus papers to grade, Christmas cookies to bake and you roped me into helping out with the Holiday Basket Drive."

"What's your point?" Olivia asked.

"My point is that dress shopping was not on my list."

Astrid pulled back the curtain then and Olivia stepped out of the dressing room.

Jamie's eyes went wide. "It's a wedding dress."

She nodded.

"It's a gorgeous wedding dress," her friend said. "But…why are you wearing a wedding dress?"

"Because I'm getting married on December 20, and I know you've got a lot going on, but I hope you can clear your schedule because I'm going to need a maid of honor."

"If I had any other plans, I'd change them," Jamie assured her. "But I don't understand. I didn't even realize you were— Wait a minute. Are you marrying the doctor?" She immediately shook her head. "No. No way. You wouldn't marry a guy I've never met."

"I'm not marrying Leo. I'm marrying Adam."

"Adam," Jamie echoed, uncomprehending.

"Your brother."

"Now I'm even more confused," her friend said. "Have you been dating my brother?"

Maybe it was a stretch to call a couple of dates (and numerous mind-blowing sexual encounters— including a couple of literal rolls in the hay) "dating," but she nodded.

This time when her friend's eyes went wide, it wasn't just with surprise but hurt. "You've been dating my brother. And you didn't tell me."

Olivia sat down beside her. "We didn't say anything to anyone, because we knew it would be awkward if things didn't work out." She managed a smile. "But things worked out."

"And fast," Jamie noted.

"I've never felt about anyone else the way I feel about your brother," she said sincerely.

"I'm going to need a minute for my head to stop spinning." Jamie drew a deep breath as she ran her hands through her hair, then let it out and looked at Olivia again. "I wondered…when I asked you to go to Las Vegas with him, if something might happen between you guys," Jamie acknowledged. "And maybe I kind of hoped that it would, finally, after so many years. I never said anything to you, but I'm not oblivious, Olivia. I figured out that you had feelings for him a long time ago. But when you got back, you didn't give any indication that anything had happened that weekend."

"Because nothing did," Olivia said. "Or maybe it did. Maybe that's when we both started to realize there was an attraction between us."

"But that was only—" Jamie paused to do a quick mental calculation "—three-and-a-half weeks ago. How did you get from an attraction to planning a wedding in three weeks?" And then, as another thought occurred to her, "Is this about Rebecca's application for custody?"

"No," Olivia immediately denied. "Or maybe yes, in that we're getting married sooner than we might otherwise have chosen to if his ex-wife wasn't trying to take the boys from Adam, but we're getting married because it's what we both want."

"Still, three weeks isn't a lot of time. Fourteen days is even less."

"Obviously it's going to be a low-key event."

"But…your book," Jamie said.

She was referring, of course, to the scrapbook Olivia had made when she was in seventh grade—combing through magazines and cutting out pictures of princess-inspired wedding gowns and cascading bouquets and elaborate, multi-tiered cakes.

"We made those books when we were in middle school, captivated by fairy tales of princesses meeting their perfectly matched princes," she reminded her friend. "But what I didn't realize then—and maybe not until Adam proposed—is that none of those details, not the dress or the flowers or the cake, matters as much as the groom."

"You really do sound like a woman in love," Jamie acknowledged.

"I really am."

"Well, you certainly picked the right dress," her friend said approvingly.

"Thank you," Olivia said. "So do you think you could spare the time to look at some bridesmaid dresses?"

"Absolutely."

"Can you show us what you've got available in a size six?" she asked Astrid. "Any shade of blue." Because blue had always been her friend's favorite color.

"Not blue," Jamie said. "Red. It's much more appropriate for a Christmas wedding, don't you think?"

Olivia couldn't hold back the smile that spread across her face. "I'm having a Christmas wedding."

"It was what you always dreamed of," Jamie noted. "With lots of Christmas trees and boughs of holly with red velvet ribbons."

"And you dreamed of getting married in Hawaii," Olivia remembered.

"Unfortunately, Thomas has too many elderly relatives who wouldn't be able to make the trip, so we're getting married here and honeymooning in Hawaii."

"Sounds like a reasonable compromise."

"But we've got lots of time to talk about that," Jamie said, waving a hand. "Today we need to focus on your wedding."

"Since we're here, I thought we could maybe spend some time looking at wedding dresses for you, too," Olivia suggested.

"I wouldn't object to that," Jamie assured her. Then she wrapped her arms around her friend and hugged her tight. "You've always been the sister-of-my-heart. Now you're going to be my sister-in-law."

Olivia hugged her back, grateful to know that she was loved by Adam's sister, if not by the man himself.

The rest of the week passed in a blur of activity. In addition to all the final details that needed to be taken care of for the wedding, there was a lot going on at school in preparation for the holiday concert before the winter break, and Olivia was making a to-do list for the weekend when Adam called Saturday morning.

"Do you have ice skates?" he asked without preamble.

"Um. Yes. At my parents' house."

"That's convenient. Because that's where we're going skating."

She had fond memories of skating on the backyard rink that her dad had made for her and her brothers when they were younger. Though he'd relinquished the task for a lot of years, he'd picked up the challenge again when Mitch married Lindsay, making him a step-grandpa to Elliott and Avenlea.

"How did this come about?" she wondered.

"Your mom called to say that your brother and sister-in-law and their kids are going to be there this after-noon to skate and she thought it would be fun if we joined them."

She heard Shirley chime in from the background. "You're going to want to put on long underwear and a warm sweater."

So Oliva put on long underwear and a warm sweater and joined Adam and his boys and the rest of her family for an impromptu skating party at the Circle G.

MG was there, too, not just with his skates on, but his old goalie pads, standing sentry in front of the hockey net while Elliott took shots on him.

"Look at where you want the puck to go," Mitch instructed his son. "That great big five-hole would be my target."

Elliott grinned and aimed for the five-hole.

MG dropped to the ice to close the gap, but not quickly enough. The puck snuck past him and into the net.

Olivia had no doubt that her brother could have stopped the shot, but he understood that building Elliott's confidence was as important as honing his wrist shot.

"Sticks and pucks away now," Lindsay said.

"Five more minutes?" Elliott pleaded.

"You've already had five more minutes," his mom told him. "And the rest of us want to be able to skate with-out having to worry about errant pucks flying around."

With a heavy sigh, Elliott gave his stick up to his dad while MG pushed the net off the ice.

The boy's disappointment was completely forgotten when Adam showed up a few minutes later with Easton, Hudson and Colton. Olivia's brothers had been taken aback to learn that Olivia was engaged to a man they hadn't even known she was dating, but they were warm and welcoming to Adam's sons. They even helped tie skates and snap on helmets, and MG showed an impressive amount of patience answering Colton's endless question about his goalie equipment leading to a tentative request to try on the glove and blocker.

Of course, MG said *yes*, immediately making him a hero in the eyes of Adam's youngest son.

When they finally got on the ice, Olivia was surprised to discover that the boys were all fairly good skaters.

"I can't do early morning hockey practices, but I can usually manage a couple of Sunday afternoon skates at the community center every month," Adam explained.

Sunday afternoons that he would probably prefer to spend relaxing at home, though she wasn't at all surprised that he'd give up R&R for his boys, because he was that kind of dad.

"Someone else has been practicing her skating skills," Olivia noted, as Avenlea lapped them.

"I don't even try to keep up anymore," Lindsay, several strides behind her daughter, confided.

"Is she still planning to start figure-skating lessons in the New Year?"

"Mitch picked up the skates I'd ordered for Christmas from the specialty shop in Battle Mountain just three days ago. At dinner that night, she announced that she wants to play hockey instead."

"Are you going to let her?" Adam asked.

"I'm never going to tell my daughter she can't do something her brother gets to do," Lindsay told him.

"So when is Mitch going back to Battle Mountain to trade the figure skates for hockey skates?" Olivia asked.

"I'm not," Mitch said, gliding up beside them. "Because I think it's important for Avenlea to try both before she makes a final decision one way or the other."

"Which means that you'll be spending a lot of time at the rink next winter, because I'm not carting…"

"A baby?" Olivia filled in helpfully, when her sister-in-law's words trailed off.

"So much for keeping the news to ourselves for a while," Mitch noted dryly.

"I didn't say anything," his wife protested.

"You didn't have to," Olivia said. "Mom figured it out on Thanksgiving."

"How?" Mitch asked.

She shrugged. "Maybe the fact that she had three kids of her own has given her some insights."

"Can I offer congratulations?" Adam asked cautiously.

"Yes, but quietly, please," Lindsay said. "We haven't told Elliott and Avenlea yet."

"They're going to be thrilled," Olivia predicted.

"I hope so," her sister-in-law said. "But no doubt Elliott will want a brother and Avenlea will want a sister, and one of them is going to be disappointed and it will somehow be my fault."

"And then we'll try again to even the odds," Mitch told her.

"Spoken like someone who doesn't have to waddle around pregnant and then push a baby out of his body," Lindsay grumbled good-naturedly.

"I had a job to do, too," Mitch reminded his wife.

"But I'm not griping about it. And I don't recall hearing any complaints from you at the time, either."

"Too much information," Olivia said, lifting her mittened hands to cover her ears.

Of course, that was the exact moment that her blade hit a bump in the ice, causing her to stumble forward, flail her arms in a desperate attempt to regain her balance, overcorrect and go down hard on her butt.

After everyone was tired out from skating—the adults, not surprisingly, packing it in before the kids—they all piled into Angela's kitchen for mugs of hot cocoa and freshly baked cookies.

"My butt is going to be sore tomorrow," Olivia grumbled to Adam, as she added a handful of miniature marshmallows to her hot cocoa.

Adam rubbed her bottom gently. "You only fell once."

"That was enough," she assured him.

"And I don't think your butt hurts as much as your pride."

He was right.

Because it wasn't just that she'd fallen, but that all of the kids had hurried across the ice to make sure that she was okay. Colton had even offered her the use of his helmet, suggesting that she might need it more than he did.

"So why are you rubbing my butt?" she challenged.

"Because I can't rub your pride." He winked. "At least not with your family watching."

"And I've given them enough to talk about today," she noted dryly.

He chuckled softly.

"At least my mom's too busy with her grandkids and soon-to-be grandkids to be fussing over me."

"Your mom *and* dad have been wonderful to my boys."

"I know I'm the one who'll be changing my name when we get married, but in their eyes, as soon as you put that ring on my finger, those boys became Gilmores as much as they're Morgans."

Not that she was wearing the ring right now, because Adam had taken it to the local jewelry store to be re-sized. But the mere fact that he'd formally proposed and given her his grandmother's ring made everything so much more real. Of course, in ten days, it was going to get even more real. And she couldn't wait.

"Did you have fun skating?" Shirley asked, when they'd returned to Morgan's Glen.

"We had. So. Much. Fun," Easton chanted.

"An' we had cookies an' cocoa," Colton added.

"And you should see their Christmas tree," Hudson told her. "It's huge! And it's got, like, a gazillion lights on it."

"A gazillion? That's a whole lot of lights."

"My parents do go a little overboard with the deco-rating," Olivia admitted.

"How come they've got a Christmas tree already?" Easton asked.

"They always get a tree the first weekend in Decem-ber, so they have lots of time to enjoy it before the holi-days," she explained.

"We should do that," Hudson decided.

"We've already missed the first weekend in December," Adam said. "But I guess there's no reason we couldn't go get a tree today."

"Today?" Easton echoed.

"Today!" Colton clapped his hands together.

"Will you come with us?" Hudson asked Olivia.

"I wouldn't miss it," she assured him.

Though she'd participated in the ritual with her own family for as far back as she could remember, this was the first time she was going to pick out a tree with anyone else. And not just anyone, but the man she was going to marry and his three adorable children and their grandmother. Her soon-to-be family.

"Yay!" Colton clapped his hands again.

"Mom?" Adam prompted, as the boys hurried to put on all the outdoor gear they'd taken off only a short while earlier.

"Oh, you kids go on without me," she said, waving a hand. "It's too cold outside for these old bones."

"Your old bones didn't have a problem last year."

"But they're a year older this year," she pointed out.

Adam shrugged. "Come on, boys. Let's go to the barn to dig out the toboggan."

"Why do you need a toboggan?"

The four Morgan men turned to stare at her.

"Have you never cut down your own Christmas tree before?" Adam asked incredulously.

"Every year," she assured him.

"At the Circle G?"

"Of course."

"And how did you get the tree back to the house?"

"We tied it to the back of one of the ATVs."

"Well, this isn't the Circle G," he reminded her. "We

have one ATV, and we use it for work, not for pleasure. Plus, there's no way we'd all fit on it, so we hike out to the woods, chop down a tree and drag it back on the sled."

"We used to get to ride on the sled to the woods," Easton confided. "But Dad said we're too big for that now."

"Or at least too heavy when all three of you are on the sled," Adam clarified.

"So now only Colton gets to ride," Hudson said. "Because he's the smallest."

"Are you coming?" Adam asked, when Olivia paused at the door.

She nodded. "I'll be right there as soon as I find my mittens."

His gaze dropped to the pockets of her coat, where he could clearly see her mittens poking out. But he only shrugged and said, "Don't take too long—it's going to be dark soon."

"I won't," she promised, already rummaging in the bin inside the closet labeled "hats, mitts, scarves" and pulling out appropriate items for Adam's mom.

Shirley frowned. "I already told Adam that I'm not going."

"He'll be happy to know that you've changed your mind."

"But I haven't changed my mind," her future mother-in-law insisted.

"Do you really want to disappoint your grandsons by missing out on one of their favorite holiday traditions?"

"They won't be disappointed," Shirley said.

"They will," she insisted. "And it will be my fault."

"What do you mean?"

"I've lost track of the number of times that the boys have told me 'Gramma always goes with us to pick out the tree.' And now, suddenly, you don't want to go and they're going to figure out that it's because I'm here."

"It's not that I don't want to go," Shirley protested. "I just think it's time for you and Adam to make new traditions with the boys, and I don't want to get in the way of that."

"You're not in the way of anything," Olivia said sincerely. "And I think they'd like to keep the old tradition—isn't that what a tradition is, after all?"

Shirley sighed and began to wind the scarf around her throat. "If I'm coming, I'm going to want my long coat."

Olivia smiled and reached into the closet.

As they trudged across the snow—a man, a woman, three boys and their grandmother in search of a Christmas tree—Olivia's heart was so full of joy that it was overflowing.

If only there wasn't the threat of a custody hearing hanging over their heads, everything would be perfect.

Chapter Eighteen

Adam had always done his best to make the holidays fun for his boys, but somewhere along the line—probably coinciding with the end of his marriage—they'd stopped being fun for him. In recent years, even decorating the tree had become just one more task to do at the end of a day filled with too many other tasks.

Until this year.

Until Olivia.

He had no doubt that he was getting the better end of the deal in marrying her. And while she didn't seem to have any concerns about what she was giving up, he really wished he hadn't had to ask her to be part of his plan to hold on to custody of his sons.

Of course, he hadn't actually asked in the first place. It had been her idea. Or rather her interpretation of his sister's idea.

And now that their plan was in motion, he wasn't sorry.

How could he be sorry when being around Olivia somehow managed to make every day a little bit brighter?

As was evidenced by the fact that his boys were currently "Rockin' Around the Christmas Tree" to the music spilling out of Olivia's iPhone.

They'd been on the go since early morning, and yet they showed no signs of slowing down. Not for the first time, he wished he could bottle some of their seemingly endless energy. Of course, getting the tree was always a sign that Christmas was just around the corner, so it was no wonder that they were excited.

The LeAnn Rimes version of the classic tune was followed by Carrie Underwood singing "Hark! The Herald Angels Sing," when Shirley interrupted with a request for everyone to wash up for dinner. While they'd been hauling boxes of decorations down from the attic, she'd been busy in the kitchen, making her oven-fried buttermilk chicken legs with roasted potatoes and crisp spinach. The meal was a favorite of her son and grandsons, and Olivia became an immediate fan, too.

After dinner, Adam and Olivia had taken care of the dishes while Gramma and the boys resumed the tree-trimming. The boys each had their own and favorite ornaments that they hung on the branches. Colton put all of his at his eye level, which was the bottom third of the tree; Easton reached up as high as he could, because it was higher than either of his brothers could reach; and Hudson generally filled in the spaces in between.

When the tree was finally finished, Adam hustled the boys upstairs for an abbreviated version of their usual bedtime routine—which Colton insisted had to include "Miz Gi-mow" reading him a story. By that time, Shirley was ready for her story time, too, and wished everyone "good night" before heading to her bed.

"I had a lengthy to-do list for this weekend," Olivia confided to him when they were finally alone. "I didn't check a single item off it today, and I'm not even a little bit sorry."

"You had a good day?"

"I had *the best* day."

He smiled at her enthusiastic response. He'd thought it was pretty great, too. He hadn't taken a whole day to hang out with his kids and have fun in…a really long time.

Well, they'd had some fun together in Vegas—sightseeing and mini-putting and swimming. But he wasn't sure that counted, since he'd been resentful about having to make the trip. And he suspected it was Olivia's presence even then that had turned an obligation into something much more pleasurable.

And now, snuggling close to her on the sofa while snow was falling outside and a fire crackled behind the grate, with the lights of the freshly cut and decorated Christmas tree glowing, he would argue that if today had been *the best* day, this was the very best part.

There had been one little snag earlier. A moment when he'd found his mom near tears as they were unboxing decorations, because she couldn't find Jamie's Christmas stocking.

Where was Jamie's Christmas stocking?

He'd quietly reminded her that Jamie had taken her

stocking—and all her favorite decorations—when she'd moved to her own house in town, several years earlier.

Shirley had looked stricken, though Adam wasn't sure if it was by the news that her daughter no longer lived with her or that she'd somehow forgotten that fact. But Olivia had come to the rescue, asking Shirley to share some of her favorite memories of Christmases with Adam and Jamie when they were little. His mom had happily taken her lead, and the potential crisis had been averted.

"Tell me about this list of yours," he said, putting his arms around Olivia now. "Was I on it?"

She tipped her head back to look at him. "My to-do list?"

"Yeah. Am I one of the things that you had to do this weekend?"

Her lips curved. "I'd put you under the heading of things I *want* to do rather than *have* to do."

"So maybe that's something we could cross off your list," he suggested hopefully.

She lifted her hands to link them behind his head and draw his mouth down to hers. "Why don't we take a walk out to the barn? Just so the day's not a total write-off."

Olivia had gotten in the habit of stopping by Morgan's Glen almost every day, because if more than twenty-four hours went by and she didn't get to see Adam and the boys, she missed them like crazy. Of course, Hudson was in her class, and she usually crossed paths with Easton and Colton at school, too. But there she was "Miss Gilmore"—though soon to be "Mrs. Morgan"—while at the ranch she was "Olivia"—soon to be Adam's wife and the boys' stepmom and Shirley's daughter-in-law.

She'd stayed away on Sunday, determined to scratch at least a few tasks off the to-do list she'd neglected on Saturday, which meant that she was twice as eager to see Adam on Monday. As she turned into the long drive on her way to the house, she saw the flag was up on the mailbox and so stopped to collect the contents before continuing on her way.

"You've got mail," she told Adam, dropping the pile of envelopes on the counter.

Most of them were likely Christmas cards, but there was one with an official-looking seal in the upper left corner that gave her pause.

"And it looks like there's something from the courthouse."

The easy smile that had been on Adam's face when he came into the kitchen to greet her faded. He picked up the envelope, staring at the seal of the District Court, Haven County, Nevada.

"There was a message on my voice mail from Katelyn's office Friday afternoon," he said, suddenly remembering. "But I haven't had a chance to call back."

"Maybe you should call now," Olivia suggested cautiously.

"Or maybe I should open the letter," he said, turning it over to peel open the flap, pretending a nonchalance she knew he didn't feel. "It's probably just a notice of a court date."

And while she hoped he was right, hope didn't prevent her stomach from twisting into knots as he unfolded the pages and began to read.

After what seemed like forever but was probably no more than two minutes, he handed the document to her.

The front page bore the heading District Court, Haven County, Nevada, followed by the names of the applicant and the respondent and a case number. Skimming further, she got to the important stuff:

IT IS HEREBY ORDERED that the previous order granting full custody of the aforementioned minor children to the respondent, Adam Morgan, is affirmed.

Dated at Haven County, Nevada this 9th day of December.

Signed by Arrosa M. Guevara, District Court Judge

Olivia looked up at Adam, her heart filled with cautious hope. "It's over?"

"It's over." He swept her into his arms and spun her around. "Isn't it the best Christmas present ever?"

His happiness was infectious, but Olivia still had unanswered questions.

"It is," she agreed. "But…your ex-wife doesn't exactly have a reputation for magnanimous gestures—don't you wonder why she decided to withdraw her application?"

"Does it matter? The boys get to stay here with me."

"And that's great. But I'd still like to know why she changed her mind—if only to ensure that she doesn't change it back again."

"If I had to guess, I'd say that she changed her mind

because she's going to have her hands full with a new baby in about seven months."

"Rebecca's pregnant?"

He nodded. "She told me after the babysitter debacle."

Before Olivia could respond to that, he called to the boys.

"Easton! Hudson! Colton!"

Footsteps scrambled overhead, then pounded on the stairs as the boys responded to their dad's summons.

"What's up?" Easton asked.

"Get your coats and boots on—we're going out for ice cream."

They exchanged puzzled glances.

"Ice cream before dinner?" Hudson said dubiously, certain his dad must be playing some kind of trick.

"Hmm…probably not a good idea," he acknowledged. "So let's go out for dinner and then ice cream."

Hudson turned to Olivia. "Are we really going out for dinner?"

"It would seem so," she said.

"Is Gramma coming, too?" Easton asked.

"Gramma's at the Circle G, working on wedding stuff with my mom," Olivia told him.

Adam opened his mouth as if to say something, then shook his head.

"We can talk later," he decided. "Right now, we've got celebrating to do."

"There's just something about a wedding, isn't there?" Shirley said, as she looked over the final menu for Adam and Olivia's big day.

"It's the beginning of something wonderful," Angela

agreed. "And I'm so happy our children are beginning that something together."

"I'll admit that while I hoped this was where they were heading, I didn't expect them to get there so fast."

"It is fast, but they both seem to know what they want."

"Except that they wanted to get married at town hall." Shirley shook her head. "A wedding should be more than a ceremony, it should be a celebration."

"Absolutely," Angela said. "But why do I think you've got something more on your mind than just wedding plans?"

"Christmas is coming up fast, too," she told her friend.

"You're hedging."

She sighed, because it was true.

"Adam's worried about me," she finally confided. "And I hate knowing that he's preoccupied with concerns about me when there are so many more important things to focus on—like his wedding and Christmas."

"Why do you think he's worried about you?" Angela asked.

"There have been a few occasions recently when I feel thoughts slipping from my mind, and no matter how hard I try, they're gone before I can catch them."

"Sounds like it's maybe something you should talk to your doctor about."

"Maybe. And maybe I'm afraid of what she might tell me."

"It's natural to be afraid, but you can't plan a course of action unless you know what you're dealing with."

She was quiet for a moment, then confided, "My mother had dementia."

"I remember." Angela's gaze was filled with compassion.

Shirley's throat grew tight. "I don't want to end up like her, not able to remember my own family."

"No one wants to end up like that," her friend said gently. "But just as you never stopped loving your mom, your family won't stop loving you, no matter what happens."

Shirley swiped at an errant tear that spilled onto her cheek.

Angela reached across the table to give her hand a squeeze. "Make an appointment to see your doctor," she urged. "And if Adam and Jamie aren't available, let me know so that I can be there with you."

"You'd really do that?"

"Of course," Angela said. "After all, we're family now—and family sticks together. Always."

When they got back to Morgan's Glen after their celebratory dinner, it was late—especially for a school night. Although Olivia had a busy week planned at school, she was happy to stick around to help with the boys' bedtime routine, happy to know that she was already accepted as part of Adam's family.

She still marveled over the fact that she'd shared her first kiss with Adam in November and would be married to him in December. Some of her coworkers had expressed concern about the whirlwind nature of her romance when they learned of her upcoming nuptials, and maybe it did seem as if everything was happening fast. Because when Olivia and Adam exchanged vows in the beautiful, whitewashed barn at Eberley Gardens, they would have been together a little more than four weeks.

Of course, Olivia had been secretly in love with her soon-to-be husband for almost fifteen years before the start of those weeks. And though she didn't like having to keep her feelings locked up inside, she knew that Adam wasn't ready to hear her say the words. And she didn't want him to feel bad if he wasn't ready to say them back to her. Though he'd denied being wary about opening his heart, she knew that he was. But she also felt confident that he was starting to open it to her.

It was going to take some more time for him to get to where she was—ready to acknowledge and declare her feelings for him—but she didn't mind. Because they were going to have their whole lives together.

Besides, she had a more immediate concern tonight.

"Can you give me a minute with Easton?" she asked Adam, after they'd said their good-nights to Colton and Hudson.

"Is something wrong?"

"You didn't notice that he was quiet at dinner?" she asked, surprised because he was usually so attuned to all of his sons' moods.

"I figured that was just because he was scarfing down his cheeseburger and fries *and* a hot-fudge sundae."

"Even growing boys sometimes have growing pains," she said lightly.

"Should I be there when you talk to him?"

"I've got this," she said, mentally crossing her fingers that it was true.

So Adam went downstairs and she went to knock on Easton's door.

"Yeah?"

That was probably as close to an invitation as she was going to get, so she pushed open the door and stepped inside.

Easton was under the covers, his bedside lamp on, a book open in front of his face.

"I thought you might want to talk," she said.

"About what?" he asked, without looking up from the book.

"Whatever's bothering you."

"No."

"Okay." She sat down on the carpeted floor, with her back to the wall so that she was facing his bed, her legs stretched out in front of her, feet crossed at the ankles.

Easton lowered the book enough that she could see his scowl. "So why are you still here?"

"Just in case you change your mind."

"I'm not gonna change my mind."

"Okay," she said again.

He stuck his nose back in his book, pretending to read. But she knew he wasn't focused on the story, because after five minutes, he hadn't turned a single page.

So maybe, if he didn't want to talk, he'd at least be willing to listen.

"There's been a lot of upheaval in your life recently," she acknowledged. "It's understandable that you'd be upset or frustrated or mad. Or maybe you're feeling so many different things that you're not entirely sure how you're feeling, and that's okay, too."

"You don't know anything about how I feel."

"Maybe not, but I'm here if you want to tell me."

"I don't."

The kid was stubborn, she'd give him that.

But she also knew that he was hurting, and that was why she couldn't walk away.

"I imagine this whole custody battle between your mom and your dad was pretty confusing," she said. "And frustrating, because no one asked you what you wanted. And scary, because change is often scary.

"But now you know that nothing's going to change, not really. And you should feel relieved, because that's what you wanted—for everything to be the way it's always been. But I bet there's a part of you that wonders why your mom started all of this only to give it up."

Easton looked at her then, his eyes shiny.

"I can't answer that question for you," she said gently. "But what I can tell you—what I know for certain, without a shadow of a doubt—is that your mom loves you and your brothers a whole lot. Maybe she doesn't express it in the ways you might want her to, but love is more than just words—it's all the little things that somebody does to show you that they care."

Easton considered that for a minute before he responded. "You're telling me to focus on her actions instead of her words?"

"I'm saying that you need to look at the whole picture—not just one day or event."

"Like the fact that she walked out on us when Colton was a baby? And was a no-show for my championship soccer game? And completely forgot Hudson's birthday last year? Or how about the fact that she suddenly decided fighting for me and Hudson and Colton wasn't worth the trouble?"

Olivia rose from the floor to perch on the edge of

the mattress. "Do you *want* to live with your mom and stepdad?"

"No!"

His response was as immediate as it was vehement, and she exhaled a shaky sigh of relief.

"But…why doesn't she want us?"

His voice cracked on the question, and so did Olivia's heart.

Then he launched himself toward her, pressing his face into her sweater and sobbing his heart out. Olivia wrapped her arms around him, holding him while he cried, until there were no tears left.

"I don't believe your mom doesn't want you," she said gently. "I think what happened is that she realized there was something she wanted even more than she wanted you to live with her—and that was for you and your brothers to be happy. And she knows you're happy here with your dad and your grandma."

"And you," Easton said, tightening his arms around her.

Now Olivia's eyes filled with tears.

"And me," she agreed. "And there isn't anywhere in the world that I would rather be."

"Because you love my dad." His tone was both matter-of-fact and hesitant, as if he wasn't quite as certain as he wanted to sound.

Olivia drew back a little, brushing the tears off his cheeks with her fingertips and forcing him to meet her gaze.

"Because I love all of you," she told him firmly. "Your dad and you and Hudson and Colton and your grandma, too."

"Really?"

She nodded. "With my whole heart. And when your dad and I get married, I won't just be making promises to him, I'll be making them to you and your brothers, too. I will be here for you and Hudson and Colton, in good times and in bad, and nothing—*absolutely nothing*—could ever make me stop loving you."

"Cross your heart?"

She crossed her heart, happy to be able to give him that little bit of comfort and reassurance. And even happier to know that, in only a few weeks, she'd be able to proudly call him her stepson.

Chapter Nineteen

"Everything okay?" Adam asked, when Olivia made her way back downstairs again.

"Yeah," she said. "It's just been an emotional day for everyone."

Her phone chimed with a message.

"Sorry," she apologized automatically. "That was just a scheduled reminder about my final dress fitting tomorrow."

"Actually...that's what I wanted to talk to you about."

She frowned. "My dress fitting?"

He hesitated. "The wedding."

An uneasy feeling started to churn in her belly. "What about the wedding?"

"Well, now that Rebecca's withdrawn her application for custody, there's no reason for us to get married."

The words pummeled Olivia's chest like physical

blows, stealing her breath. "You want to call off the wedding?"

"It makes sense, don't you think?" He seemed oblivious to the fact that he was trampling her heart into dust beneath his boots. "We were getting married to make a stronger case for the boys to stay with me, but that's all settled now."

He was understandably ecstatic that the legal battle for his children was over. And she was happy about that, too. Sincerely. She just hadn't realized, after everything they'd shared over the past few weeks, that their entire relationship was still predicated upon Rebecca's custody application.

Her own fault, she acknowledged now. Adam had been clear from the start that he wasn't going to fall in love with her. But she'd foolishly let herself hope that his feelings for her would grow over time. She'd certainly never considered that he'd back out of their plan.

"I know you spent a lot of time picking out your dress and flowers and stuff. We all got caught up in the excitement of planning the wedding. But I'll be honest, I'm relieved that we don't have to go through with it."

"Relieved?" she echoed numbly.

"I was never comfortable knowing that you were sacrificing your future for me and the boys," he clarified.

"I never felt that marrying you would be a sacrifice."

On the contrary, starting a life with the man she loved would have been the culmination of a longtime dream.

"I know. And I'm grateful to you for that," he said. "But now you'll be free to go out and meet new people, to find that special someone you've been looking for and finally fall in love."

Could he really be unaware of her feelings—even after all this time?

The earnest expression on his face seemed to support that assumption. It was as if he honestly believed he was doing her a favor by breaking their engagement, completely oblivious to the fact that he was also breaking her heart.

Well, she wasn't going to let him find solace in ignorance a moment longer.

"I haven't been waiting to fall in love," she told him. "I've been in love this whole time—with you."

He took a step back, his jaw going slack.

Yep. Completely oblivious.

He finally managed to close his mouth, then opened it again to speak. "Olivia—"

"I know you told me not to fall in love with you," she said. "But when you said those words, it was already too late. You asked me in Vegas about the first boy I ever loved. That boy was you. I fell for you when I was fifteen and I've loved you ever since.

"But even if I hadn't fallen in love with you then, there's no way I could have stopped those feelings from developing now. Because you are everything I've ever wanted, Adam Morgan—a good man, a devoted son, a loyal brother, a patient father, a thoughtful friend and a spectacular lover."

"Olivia—"

"Don't say it," she pleaded. "Don't tell me you don't feel the same way. I know you only asked me to marry you because you didn't want to lose your boys, but whether or not you can bring yourself to say the words, I know you have feelings for me."

"Of course I have feelings for you," he told her. "You're an amazing woman and a good friend, and...I care about you. But I told you from day one that I wasn't going to fall in love with you, and I refuse to feel guilty because you want something now that I told you from the beginning that I couldn't give to you."

"There's a difference between *can't* and *won't*," she said. "I know you're capable of feeling love and that you do, because I see it in your interactions with Easton, Hudson and Colton and your mom and even your sister."

His expression was regretful, his tone gentle. "I never wanted to hurt you, Olivia."

She swallowed. "Yet here we are."

And she knew that if she didn't leave right now, she was going to completely fall apart. And maybe it was silly to want to hold on to her pride, but at the moment, it was the only thing she had left.

She shoved her arms into her coat and grabbed her purse off the table. "Don't forget that you promised to decorate gingerbread houses with the boys after school tomorrow."

And it broke her heart all over again to realize that she would miss not just that but so many other things that they'd talked about doing over the holidays. And she suspected that the boys weren't going to be too happy about the change of plans, either.

But that was for Adam to deal with now.

"I know they're expecting you to be here for the decorating," he said. "So if you want—"

"No," she said, fighting desperately against the tears

that burned her eyes. "Don't you dare pretend that any of this is about what *I* want."

She'd never been one for big dramatic scenes, but she almost wished she had a ring on her finger, so she could take it off and throw it at him now. But the day after his official proposal, he'd taken his grandmother's ring to the local jeweler to be resized and hadn't yet gotten it back.

So instead of tossing a diamond, she tossed her hair over her shoulder and walked out.

Decorating gingerbread houses was one of their holiday traditions that Adam knew his boys really looked forward to each year. Of course, that might be because they put more candy in their mouths than on their respective houses, but the annual event was usually as much fun as it was messy.

The gingerbread houses that Olivia had preassembled were set around the table, with three bags of icing and half a dozen little bowls filled with various types of candy for decorating.

"We can't start without Olivia," Hudson said. "When is she going to get here?"

"Olivia isn't coming over today," Adam told them.

"Why not?" Easton demanded.

"Because the gingerbread houses are something we do together—just you guys and me."

"An' Gwamma," Colton chimed in.

"Yes, sometimes Gramma helps," Adam agreed. "But she's part of our family."

"And Olivia's gonna be part of our family, too," Hudson reminded him. "You're gonna get married and then she's gonna be our stepmom."

Hudson's words were a kick in Adam's gut. He should have been prepared for this. He should have known the boys would have questions. But he'd thought—*hoped*—that they'd be happy enough to have the status quo restored and accept Olivia's absence from their lives as easily as they'd accepted her presence.

"Can we just decorate the gingerbread houses now and talk about Olivia later?"

"Why?" Easton asked, his gaze narrowed suspiciously.

"Because there's a lot of candy that needs to be put on these houses."

Colton dutifully picked up his bag of icing and began to squeeze it onto the roof of his house.

"Is Olivia coming over later?" Easton asked. "For family movie night?"

"No," Adam admitted.

"But it's her turn to pick the movie," Hudson said.

"She has other things to do tonight," he hedged.

And the way Easton's gaze narrowed, he knew his dad was hedging. "What kind of other things?"

"I don't know, exactly. But...I know Olivia isn't going to be coming around as much anymore." Or ever.

"But why?" Easton's voice broke on the question. "She told me—she *promised*—that she would be here for us."

"*I'm* here for you," he reminded his boys. "Just like I've always been. And we've been doing just fine for the last four and a half years, haven't we? You guys and me and Gramma."

"Maybe," Easton allowed. "But we were doing better with Olivia."

"I know you guys are disappointed—"

"Disappointed?" Easton stared him down, looking a lot less like the nine-year-old boy he was and more like the man he would someday be. "Disappointed is... it's how you feel when you're looking forward to a blue raspberry slushie at the movies but they only have green apple. We're not *disappointed,* we're..."

He trailed off, as if he didn't quite know how to describe what he was feeling. Instead, he curled his hand into a fist and smashed it down on the roof of his gingerbread house.

"Easton!" Adam was shocked by the violence of his son's action, stricken by the heartbreak on his son's face. Unfortunately, he knew that he had no one but himself to blame. He'd been so desperate to hold on to his family, he hadn't considered the potential repercussions of his plan—or of changing that plan. "I know you're hurting, and I'm sorry, but—"

His eldest son cut him off again. "We're hurting because of *you.*" He punched the broken house again. "*You* told us Olivia was going to be our stepmom." Again. "*You* let us love her." And again. "And then *you* sent her away."

Easton stormed off then, leaving a pile of cookie pieces and crumbs where his gingerbread house once stood.

Adam didn't protest when Hudson followed his brother out of the room. Instead, he turned his attention to his youngest son.

Colton was still seated at the table, holding the icing

bag, white frosting now dripping from the tip to puddle on the table. But it was the tears sliding down his cheeks that made a complete mess of Adam's heart.

"What are you doing here?" Angela asked, when Olivia walked into the kitchen as her parents were finishing up dinner Tuesday night. "I thought you had an appointment at Bliss tonight."

"I canceled it." Her tone was uncharacteristically short.

"I know your dress seemed to fit perfectly the last time you tried it on, but it's not uncommon for brides to lose a few pounds in the lead-up to the wedding and—"

"Angela," Charles interrupted his wife gently. "Let Olivia talk."

Her mom pressed her lips together.

"Come have a seat and tell us what's on your mind," her dad invited.

Olivia hesitated for just a moment before lowering herself into her usual seat at the table.

She looked from her mom to her dad, then at the hands she'd folded together as she said, "The wedding's off."

Angela gasped. "Off? What do you mean *off*?"

She'd known that her parents would be disappointed when she broke the news, and she hated having to tell them, but she hated even more that it was true. That the wedding she'd dreamed of, to the only man she'd ever loved, wasn't going to happen.

"I mean that Adam and I aren't getting married."

"But—"

"Angela," Charles interrupted again. "Can you give me and Olivia a moment?"

"But," she began again, then sighed and pushed away from the table.

"I'm sorry," Olivia whispered, when she and her dad were alone.

"Why are you apologizing?"

"Because I know you and mom are disappointed—"

"We're disappointed *for* you—not disappointed *in* you," he said. "You have never made us anything but proud."

She felt the sting of tears in her eyes.

"Do you want to tell me what happened?"

"He just…changed his mind."

Of course, it was more complicated than those few words implied, but in the end, that was what had happened. Realizing that he didn't need a wife, Adam had decided that he didn't want one. That he didn't want her.

"Do you want me to go kick his ass?"

Olivia choked on a laugh. "I don't know that that would solve anything."

"It might make me feel better." He leaned across the table to gently brush a tear from her cheek. "Now I really want to kick his ass, because he made my little girl cry."

"Your little girl is a grown woman," she reminded him.

"And your tears make me ache just as much now as they did when you were a child. Maybe more," he said. "Because I know this is something I can't fix with a kiss and a Band-Aid."

"It might help if you told me that he's not worth my tears," she said.

"I don't think it would," Charles denied. "Because I know how much you love him, and I have to believe that he's going to come to his senses and realize he loves you too much to let you go."

Olivia wished she could believe it, too, but she'd already spent far too many years and far too many wishes on Adam Morgan.

Shirley surveyed the broken gingerbread and candies scattered across the kitchen table.

"What happened here?"

"The decorating didn't quite go as planned," he admitted.

"You told the boys that you called off the wedding?" she guessed.

Adam frowned. "I didn't tell *you* that I called off the wedding." Of course, he'd intended to. He just hadn't gotten around to it yet.

"I know my thoughts sometimes get muddled, but there's nothing wrong with my hearing," she told him.

He scrubbed his hands over his face. "When I found out that Rebecca had withdrawn her custody application, I was…overjoyed. And so certain it meant that everything was going to be okay. That the status quo had been restored."

"Apparently the boys weren't as happy with the status quo as you were."

"I guess I underestimated how much they like Olivia."

"They *love* Olivia," Shirley said. "And why wouldn't

they? She's smart and beautiful and warm and fun and—"

"I get it," Adam said. "And you're right. She's great. But I'm not going to marry her just because it's what the boys want me to do."

"And you shouldn't," his mom agreed. "You should marry her because you love her."

"Except that I don't," he said bluntly. "The only reason Olivia and I planned to get married was to ensure I didn't lose the boys."

If his mom was surprised by his confession, she didn't show it. Instead, she shook her head and said, "This is my fault."

"What are you talking about?" he asked, wondering if her mind had drifted again.

"I raised a fool."

"Excuse me?"

"Maybe you thought your relationship with Oliva was about the boys. Maybe that's what you needed to tell yourself to open up and let her in. But it's time to face the truth. To own up to your true feelings, Adam."

"Mom. I'm not in love with Olivia," he insisted.

"A fool so deep in denial he's on the verge of drowning," she declared.

"You're being a little melodramatic, don't you think?"

"What I think is that you were a lot happier with Olivia than you are now. You smiled more easily and laughed more freely."

"Maybe that wasn't Olivia but an overload of dopamine because we were having sex all the time."

"If you're trying to shock me, you failed," she said. "And the fact that you enjoyed an intimate relationship

with Olivia is only further proof of the connection between you."

"Sometimes sex is just sex, Mom."

"And sometimes a man is so intent on protecting
himself from potential hurt that he doesn't realize the
greatest danger is himself."

"I'm not even going to pretend I know what that
means," he told her.

"Then you're a bigger fool than I thought."

"I'm sorry if you don't approve of my decision, but
it's my life and my decision to make."

"You're right," she said. "But you're not the only one
who has to live with the consequences—your sons do,
too. And while they seem to know that means living
without Olivia, I don't think that reality has sunk in
for you yet."

Somehow Olivia managed to get through the next
day. She'd been tempted to take a personal day—or
even several personal days—so that she could stay in
bed until the New Year. Because at least while she was
sleeping, she wasn't thinking about the fact that all of
her dreams had been within her grasp—or that now
they were gone, leaving an emptiness inside her that was
huge and excruciatingly painful. But she couldn't aban-
don her students to a substitute so close to the holiday.

As soon as her last student was out the door Wednesday afternoon, though, so was she. Eager to escape before she could be cornered by a colleague who might
want to chat about the holiday concert or the last day of
school assembly—or her upcoming wedding.

It was inevitable, of course, that they would find out

what happened. That her groom had called things off only eight days before the wedding. And she'd answer all of their questions when she returned to school in the New Year, but right now, Olivia needed some time to tend to her broken heart.

To figure out how this had happened.

Maybe it was her own fault. Maybe she'd put too much focus on the idea of a wedding instead of the man, because if she'd been content to stick with their original plan of a quick ceremony at town hall, then she and Adam would have been married two weeks ago, and the fact that Rebecca had decided to drop her custody suit wouldn't have changed anything. Because it was a lot easier to say "let's call off the wedding" than "let's get a divorce."

Not that she wanted Adam to stay with her because it was easy. She wanted him to want to be with her—because he loved her.

Except that he didn't.

And she really had no right to be heartbroken over that realization when he'd told her from the very beginning that he wasn't going to fall in love with her. And she'd told him that she was going into the relationship with her eyes wide open.

She was the one who'd lied.

So if she was looking to blame someone for the fact that her heart was shattered into a million pieces, she only had to look in a mirror.

Instead she asked Alexa to turn on her Christmas tree lights and play some holiday music. Because it really wasn't in her nature to wallow in self-pity and she refused to let any man—even one she'd loved for half her life—ruin the holidays for her.

And the truth was, her life right now really wasn't that much different than it had been four weeks earlier—before he'd ever kissed her.

But *she* was different now.

Because she'd been kissed by Adam Morgan.

Because she'd not only made love with him but also made plans for a future with him.

Because he'd given her the greatest gift in allowing her to be part of his family, if only for a little while.

And, yeah, it hurt like hell now that he'd taken that gift back, but she would survive and she would move on.

It would take some time, but she would move on with her life, without him.

So after she spent a few hours updating her lesson plans and to-do lists, she poured herself a bowl of cereal for dinner—because each little step was a necessary step forward—and splashed milk on the counter when she jolted in response to pounding on her door.

She peeked through the sidelight, chastising herself for the flood of disappointment when she saw that it wasn't Adam—as she'd foolishly hoped, if only for a moment—but his sister.

She twisted the dead bolt and pulled open the door for her friend.

"What are you doing here?"

"Making sure you aren't lying in a pool of blood," Jamie said. "Because that's the only reason I could imagine for you skipping out on the basket assembly."

Olivia winced. "Ohmygod—I completely forgot."

"You? Forgot?"

She couldn't blame her friend for sounding so skeptical. The Stoney Ridge Elementary School Holiday Basket Drive was an initiative that Olivia had spearheaded four years earlier, and though she was lucky to have a fabulous committee that was responsible for securing the donations, she *always* participated in the assembly of the baskets.

"I'm sorry."

"I know you've got a lot on your mind because you're getting married in six days, but…"

Jamie's words trailed off when her friend's eyes filled with tears.

"Oh, crap. I didn't mean to make you feel bad about missing the basket party. It was fine. We had more than enough volunteers. There's no need to cry."

Olivia could only shake her head.

"Okay, now you're scaring me," Jamie said.

"I'm sorry," Olivia said again. "I just—I wanted to be able to tell you without completely falling apart. Or maybe I assumed that he would have told you."

"Tell me *what*?"

"There isn't going to be a wedding in six days. There isn't ever going to be a wedding for me and Adam."

"What are you talking about? Just last week we were tying ribbons around votive cups for the reception."

"I'm so—"

"Stop saying you're sorry and tell me. *What. The. Hell. Happened.*"

She wanted to tell Jamie, to confide in her BFF. But when she opened her mouth again, instead of words, it was a sob that burst forth. And once the tears started, she couldn't make them stop. Not for a long time.

Eventually she told her friend everything. The truth about their very different reasons for wanting to get married. Adam's obvious relief that he didn't have to marry a woman he was never going to love.

And Olivia's certainty that she would never love anyone else.

"So there was a pool of blood," Jamie said softly. "I just didn't see it."

Olivia nodded.

"You should have called me right away," her friend said. "I would have brought Ben and Jerry to commiserate with you."

"I wanted to call you, but...he's your brother."

"You're the sister-of-my-heart," Jamie reminded her. "And my brother is a dick."

She choked on a laugh.

"Thank you," she said sincerely. "Until right now, I was certain I wouldn't ever laugh again."

Jamie put an arm around her, and Olivia let her head fall back against her shoulder.

"You're going to be okay," her friend promised.

"I *am* going to be okay," Olivia agreed. "I just needed to have a good cry before I cancel the barn and the caterer and the flowers and—"

"Let me take care of all of that wedding stuff for you," Jamie said.

"Are you sure?"

"Absolutely."

"Thank you, sister-of-my-heart."

Jamie hugged her tighter. "I love you, Liv."

And Olivia found some solace in knowing that while she might not have gotten the man of her dreams, she at least had the best friend in the world.

Chapter Twenty

His mom was right. It took a few days for the reality of living without Olivia to sink in for Adam—and when it did, that reality was pretty damn bleak.

He hadn't realized how much light she brought to his life just by being in it. And not only his life, of course, but also Easton's, Hudson's, Colton's and even Shirley's. But they'd been doing just fine before she came along, and he had to believe they'd get there again.

Except now he knew that *just fine* wasn't good enough.

Being with Olivia had shown them all that there was the possibility of something better.

For almost five years, he'd been a single dad of three boys. With Olivia, they'd become a family. She'd filled a void in their lives that he hadn't even known existed, and maybe he could live without her, but...

He didn't want to.

He didn't want to spend another minute of another day without her.

Because he loved her.

Yep, his mom had been right about that, too.

He was in love with Olivia, and he'd made a mistake—probably the biggest mistake of his life—when he let her go.

When you make a mistake, you fix it.

That was the advice that he'd always given to his boys.

But Olivia's heart wasn't a toy that could be mended with a dab of Krazy Glue, and he didn't know how he could possibly fix it—or even if she'd let him try.

Thursday's "Sounds of the Season" holiday concert was a big event for the staff and students of Stoney Ridge Elementary School, their families and the community. For Olivia, it would also be a test—the first time she'd come face-to-face with Adam after the night he ended their short-lived engagement. Because, of course, he would show up for the concert. Since Easton had started kindergarten, he hadn't missed a school event, and she knew this year wouldn't be any different.

And she didn't want it to be. She didn't want Adam to feel that he couldn't attend activities and events just because he'd broken her heart. So she would put on her favorite holiday sweater and a big smile and greet him as if he was any other parent rather than the man she'd planned to marry. The man she still loved.

She was prepared to see Adam, but she was completely taken aback when Hudson entered her classroom with his mom and stepdad.

Recovering quickly, she welcomed and thanked them for coming.

"The boys did us proud tonight," Greg said.

Olivia agreed. Easton had been one of the emcees, Hudson a Russian dancer in *The Nutcracker* montage and Colton an elf in the chorus, and all three had performed their roles admirably.

"And then Hudson lured us here with the promise of snacks and drinks."

"There are refreshments available in every classroom," Olivia said. "But Hudson knew there would be Rice Krispie squares in here—and they don't last long."

"Can I go get one?" he asked now.

"Of course."

He hurried over to the refreshment table.

"I understand congratulations are in order," Olivia said to the newlyweds, when Hudson was out of earshot.

"Thank you," Greg said. "It's still early, so we haven't told many people yet, but we're very excited."

The smile that spread across Rebecca's face was radiant. "My boys are going to have a little sister."

"And our daughter will be lucky to have three big brothers looking out for her," Greg added.

"Congratulations again," Olivia said. "And merry Christmas."

They moved on to join Hudson as Peyton dragged her grandparents over to introduce them to Miss Gilmore. Then Clive came in with his mom, followed by Addison and Isabelle and their parents. Adam and Shirley came through a short time later, while Olivia was chatting with Omar's dad, and when she turned around again, they were gone.

She decided to mark it as a win. They'd been in the same room together, there had been a moment of eye contact and she hadn't fallen to pieces.

The last lingering guests had just departed when Jamie came in and sank into one of the child-size chairs. "One more day."

"One more *fun-filled* day," Olivia clarified.

She was sincerely looking forward to the holiday activities she'd planned and grateful to be busy, because she knew that when school was out and she had time on her hands, she'd likely spend too much of that time thinking about the three boys who'd stolen her heart and the man who'd broken it.

"My class has a science test tomorrow," Jamie said.

"No wonder the kids call you 'mean Miss Morgan.'"

"Who calls me that?" Jamie demanded.

Olivia chuckled. "Nobody. You know all your kids love you—although a science test on the last day of school before the holiday might cause some of them to reassess."

"Maybe." Jamie stretched her legs out in front of her. "But tonight was good, wasn't it?"

"Really good."

"So…have you made any plans for the holidays?"

"Most of my shopping's done, but I've still got all the wrapping to do. Aside from that, I'm going to curl up in my pj's, drink lots of hot cocoa and watch too many holiday movies."

"There's no such thing as too many holiday movies," Jamie chided. "But I like your plan so much that I just might crash your party one night."

"You're welcome anytime," Olivia assured her. "But

aren't you and Thomas planning another trip to Portland over the holidays to see his family?"

"We are, but that's not happening until after Christmas."

"In that case…can I ask you a favor?"

"Anything."

"I've got some presents for the boys—after I get them wrapped, can I give them to you to deliver?"

"Are you sure you don't want to take them to Morgan's Glen yourself?"

"I'm sure," Olivia said. "It's just… I can't. It's too soon."

"I'll take them," Jamie promised. "And I'll give my brother a piece of my mind while I'm there."

Olivia finished wrapping her presents Saturday afternoon and texted Jamie to ask if she could drop off the gifts for Adam's children.

Her friend's reply was immediate:

I'm here all day.

Jamie was at the door before Olivia even had a chance to knock, pulling it open and practically dragging her friend over the threshold.

"Um. Hi."

Jamie gave her a big hug—crushing the bag of gifts between them.

"That's quite the greeting, especially considering that I saw you at school yesterday afternoon."

"I just wanted to remind you that I love you."

"I love you, too," Olivia said cautiously.

Her friend took the bag from her now and set it aside. "And if I were ever to do something that you thought was a bad idea, I hope you'd realize that it was because I love you and want what's best for you."

Olivia was starting to get an uneasy feeling. "What did you do?"

Jamie stepped to the side to reveal the three boys standing behind her.

"Oh." She was admittedly surprised—but not at all displeased—to see them. "Hi, guys."

"Hi, Miss Gilmore."

"You can call me Olivia when we're not at school," she reminded them, making an effort to keep her voice light, casual.

Colton moved forward to wrap his arms around her legs. "I wuv you, Miz Gi-mow."

So much for keeping it casual.

She pressed her lips together to hold back the sob that lodged in her throat and touched a hand to his head, her fingers stroking the soft curls. "I love you, too." She shifted her gaze to encompass Easton and Hudson, too. "All of you."

Easton was suddenly fascinated by the patterned tile on the floor and Hudson found a loose thread dangling from the cuff of his sweatshirt of great interest.

Boys will be boys, Olivia mused.

"Are you mad?" Jamie asked cautiously.

"Of course I'm not mad."

"Then come in," her friend urged, helping Olivia off with her coat. "There's no reason we all need to be crowded in the foyer."

"We brought you a present," Easton said, offering

her a small square box wrapped in festive paper and topped with a red bow.

"Oh." She hadn't expected that. "Thank you."

"Open it," Hudson said.

"You want me to open it now?"

All three heads bobbed up and down.

"I have gifts for you guys, too—"

"That will be under their tree on Christmas morning," Jamie interjected.

"That doesn't seem fair," Olivia protested, but her friend waved a hand dismissively.

She tore the bow off the package, then slid a fingernail beneath the seam of the paper.

"Will you tear the damn paper, already?" Jamie muttered.

"That's a bad wuhd, Auntie Jamie," Colton said.

"I know. Just don't tell your grandma I said it, okay?"

"It's Santa you should be worried about this time of year," Olivia told her friend. "He's the one who'll put coal in your stocking."

Colton giggled at the idea of his aunt ending up on Santa's naughty list, as Olivia finally peeled the paper away from the box, then opened the lid.

"It's a Christmas tree ornament," Hudson said, in case the ribbon looped through the top hadn't immediately given that away.

"It's a snowman!" Colton said.

"A snow-*woman*," Easton corrected.

It was a snow-woman figurine, wearing a hat that said "Mom" and a scarf with the year inscribed on the fringe, with three snow "boys" snuggled close to her.

Olivia honestly didn't know what to say, and she

wasn't sure she'd be able to get any words past the lump in her throat, anyway.

"Do you like it?" Hudson asked.

She swallowed and attempted a response. "I like it very much."

She looked at Jamie, wordlessly pleading for help.

But for once, her friend was silent.

"Dad's got a present for you, too," Easton said, just as Adam came around the corner from the kitchen.

"So—" Jamie found her voice and sprang up from her chair "—who wants cookies?"

"I do!"

"Me, too!"

"An' me!"

They hustled off to the kitchen, their voices fading a bit. And suddenly Olivia and Adam were alone.

"Don't be too mad at Jamie," Adam said. "She wasn't an entirely willing accomplice."

"You didn't need an accomplice. If you wanted to talk, you could have just called and said you wanted to talk."

"I wasn't sure if you'd answer my call," he admitted. "And I wouldn't have blamed you if you didn't."

She carefully rewrapped the Mom ornament in the tissue and closed the lid of the box. "What do you want, Adam?"

"I want you to open this," he said, offering her a smaller box wrapped similarly to the one Easton had given her.

"I don't think this is a good idea."

"Please," he said.

She reluctantly took the gift and tore off the paper

with shaking fingers, revealing a blue velvet box. Inside the box was…his grandmother's diamond ring.

"I finally got it back from the jeweler," he explained. "It should fit perfectly now, which is exactly how you fit into our lives."

"Adam—"

"I always hated the expression *broken family*." The words came out in a rush, as if he was eager to cut her off before she said something he didn't want to hear. "Sure, my marriage to Rebecca didn't work out, but that didn't mean our family was broken.

"Maybe we were unconventional," he acknowledged. "A dad, three kids and their grandmother—but we were still a family."

"Families come in all shapes and sizes," she agreed. As a teacher, she'd seen plenty of examples that proved a family didn't need to be conventional to work.

"And ours worked perfectly well just the way it was," he said. "Then you came along and somehow made it better. You filled an empty space that I didn't even realize was there—not just in our family, but in my heart."

Her eyes filled with tears—again. "This isn't fair. You can't ambush me like this and say things like that and… It's not fair."

"I can't afford to play fair," he told her. "I can't afford to lose you again."

"You didn't lose me—you sent me away."

"I was a fool. At least, that's the word my mother used."

"Your sister called you a dick."

"I wouldn't argue with that characterization, either," he said. "I made mistakes, and I'm undoubtedly going to make some more, but I hope you'll forgive me—"

he took the ring out of the box and reached for her left hand "—and give us another chance."

She curled her fingers into her palm. "I don't understand why you're doing this when there's no reason we have to get married now."

"No reason except that I love you and don't want to live another day of my life without you."

"You told me that there was no way you were ever going to fall in love with me," she reminded him.

"I was a fool, Olivia," he said again. "And a coward. Afraid to risk my heart, my family.

"I didn't love Rebecca—not the way a man should love his wife and the mother of his children. And yet, it was devastating when she left. Not because she broke my heart, but because she broke Easton's and Hudson's and Colton's, and there was no way I was ever going to let anybody close enough to do that again.

"And I didn't consciously let you in, but suddenly you were there. And maybe I realized that you were someone who did have the power to break my heart, so I sent you away rather than risk having that happen. I thought I was protecting myself and my family. Not realizing, until it was too late, that you were the only one who also had the power to heal my heart.

"You're right. We don't have to get married. But I *want* to marry you, Olivia. I want to share my life and my family with you. And I want the rest of our life together to start as soon as possible."

She brushed the backs of her hands over her cheeks, swiping at the tears that had started to fall. "That's quite the speech."

"I've spent some time working on it," he confided.

"I knew that I'd only have one shot, and I wanted to get it right." He tipped her chin up, forcing her to meet his gaze. "Please tell me I got it right."

She somehow managed to smile. "I'd give you an A."

"I'd rather you gave me a *yes*." He took her hand again. "Will you marry me, Olivia?"

"Yes," she said. "Because I love you, Adam. I've always loved you and I always will."

He kissed her then, long and slow and deep.

"What's happening?" Hudson whispered the question from the vicinity of the kitchen.

"I don't know. I can't hear them talking anymore," Easton whispered back.

"Shh," Jamie admonished.

Hudson must have snuck a peek around the corner, because he suddenly announced, "They're kissing!"

"Does that mean the wedding's back on?"

Olivia eased her lips from Adam's. "I think we're going to have to finish this later."

"I can wait. As long as I have to. As long as I'm with you."

"So—" Jamie poked her head into the living room "—is the wedding back on?"

"The wedding's back on," Adam confirmed, finally sliding the ring onto Olivia's finger.

And he was right.

It was a perfect fit.

"Yes!"

"Yay!"

"Ho-way!"

"We're going to have to pick a new date," Olivia pointed out.

"Why? Do you have other plans on the twentieth?" Adam asked teasingly.

"I don't have *any* plans for the twentieth," she told him. "Jamie canceled them—the venue, the food, the flowers."

"Actually, I didn't cancel anything," Jamie confessed. "Because I had faith that my brother would eventually figure out what was in his heart and make things right."

"That was a pretty big gamble," Olivia said.

Her friend just grinned. "You're welcome."

"Can we go home now?" Easton asked.

Adam looked at Olivia. "Will you come back to Morgan's Glen with us?"

"Of course," she agreed. "I've got a new ornament I really want to hang on our tree."

Three days later, on the twentieth of December, Charles Gilmore walked his daughter down the aisle to marry Adam Morgan. Jamie was the maid of honor, and Easton, Hudson and Colton stood at the altar beside their dad while he exchanged vows with his bride. In the front row, Angela Gilmore and Shirley Morgan were seen dabbing at happy tears as their families, long connected by friendship, were joined together in love.

Epilogue

Twelve months later

Adam walked into the living room just as Olivia finished restocking the Christmas tree with candy canes.

"Have the boys been pilfering your decorations again?" he asked.

"Yes, but thankfully only the edible ones."

He chuckled as he wrapped his arms around her.

She leaned back into his embrace. "Only one more day of school."

"You're just as bad as the kids," he chided. "Counting down to the holidays."

"And this year, we've got an anniversary to celebrate, too."

"It's hard to believe that it's been a year already," he noted.

It had been a busy year, too, with plenty of ups and downs.

In April, Shirley was officially diagnosed with early onset dementia. She'd been prescribed medication that was, thankfully, slowing the progression of the disease, but they all knew she had a difficult battle ahead, and they were preparing to fight it together.

In July, Rebecca and Greg's baby was born. While the new parents were overjoyed with their daughter, Easton, Hudson and Colton weren't impressed with the little sister who apparently didn't do anything but cry and sleep and poop. Still, the boys continued to spend every other weekend with their mom and stepdad and baby Brooklyn—which gave Adam and Olivia some time alone to enjoy being newlyweds.

In August, Jamie and Thomas were married. In the absence of her father, the bride had asked her big brother to walk her down the aisle, and he happily obliged. Of course, Olivia was the matron of honor.

"I noticed that your sister was drinking peppermint tea instead of coffee in the staff room this morning," she said to her husband now.

"And that's significant…why?"

She turned so that she was facing him. "Because she's obviously avoiding caffeine—which means she's either pregnant or hoping to be."

"If she's pregnant, I'm sure you'll be one of the first people she tells when she's ready."

"I'd better be."

"What about you?" he wondered. "Do you have any thoughts on expanding our family?"

"I know the boys would love a dog."

"I'm not asking about the boys. I'm asking about you—do you want to have a baby?"

"I've given it some thought," she admitted. "But I think our family is perfect just the way it is."

"Are you sure?" he pressed.

"I am one hundred percent certain." Olivia lifted her hands to his shoulders. "All I ever wanted was a family of my own, and the day I became your wife and stepmom to your sons, all of my dreams came true."

"Isn't that a lucky coincidence?" Adam said, dipping his head to brush his lips over hers. "Because mine did, too."

* * * * *

Look for Deacon and Sierra's story, the next installment in award-winning author Brenda Harlen's Match Made in Haven miniseries, coming soon to Harlequin Special Edition!

And catch up with the happenings in Haven, Nevada!

Don't miss

The Marine's Road Home
The Rancher's Promise
Captivated by the Cowgirl

and more!

Available now, wherever Harlequin books and ebooks are sold.

COMING NEXT MONTH FROM

HARLEQUIN®
SPECIAL EDITION™

#2947 THE MAVERICK'S CHRISTMAS SECRET
Montana Mavericks: Brothers & Broncos • by Brenda Harlen
Ranch hand Sullivan Grainger came to Bronco to learn the truth about his twin's disappearance. All he's found so far is more questions—and an unexpected friendship with his late brother's sister-in-law, Sadie Chamberlin. The sweet and earnest shopkeeper offers Sullivan a glimpse of how full his life could be, if only he could release the past and embrace Sadie's Christmas spirit!

#2948 STARLIGHT AND THE CHRISTMAS DARE
Welcome to Starlight • by Michelle Major
Madison Mauer is trying to be content with her new life working in a small town bar but is still surprised when her boss-mandated community work leads to some unexpected friendships, including a teenage delinquent. The girl's older brother is another kind of surprise—and they're all in need of some second chances this Christmas!

#2949 THEIR TEXAS CHRISTMAS MATCH
Lockharts Lost & Found • by Cathy Gillen Thacker
A sudden inheritance stipulates commitment-phobes Skye McPherson and Travis Lockhart must marry and live together for a hundred and twenty days. A quick, temporary marriage is clearly the easiest solution. Until Skye discovers she's pregnant with her new husband's baby and Travis starts falling for his short-term wife. With a million reasons to leave, will love win out this Christmas?

#2950 LIGHTS, CAMERA...WEDDING?
Sutter Creek, Montana • by Laurel Greer
Fledgling florist Bea Halloran has banked her business and love life on her upcoming reality TV Christmas wedding. When her fiancé walks out, Bea's best friend, Brody Emerson, steps in as the fake groom, saving her business...and making her feel passion she barely recognizes. And Brody's smoldering glances and knee-weakening kisses might just put their platonic vows to the test...

#2951 EXPECTING HIS HOLIDAY SURPRISE
Gallant Lake Stories • by Jo McNally
Jade is focused on her new bakery and soon, raising her new baby. When Jade's one-night stand, Trent Mitchell, unexpectedly shows up, it's obvious that their chemistry is real. Until Jade's fierce independence clashes with Trent's doubts about fatherhood. Is their magic under the mistletoe strong enough to make them a forever family?

#2952 COUNTERFEIT COURTSHIP
Heart & Soul • by Synithia Williams
When a kiss at a reality TV wedding is caught on camera, there's only one way to save *his* reputation and *her* career. Now paranormal promoter Tyrone Livingston and makeup artist Kiera Fox are officially dating. But can a relationship with an agreed-upon end date turn into a real and lasting love?

YOU CAN FIND MORE INFORMATION ON UPCOMING HARLEQUIN TITLES, FREE EXCERPTS AND MORE AT HARLEQUIN.COM.

HSECNM1022

SPECIAL EXCERPT FROM

HARLEQUIN
SPECIAL EDITION

Madison Mauer is trying to be content with her new life working in a small-town bar but is still surprised when her boss-mandated community work leads to some unexpected friendships, including a teenage delinquent. The girl's older brother is another kind of surprise—and they're all in need of some second chances this Christmas!

Read on for a sneak peek at
Starlight and the Christmas Dare,
the next book in the Welcome to Starlight miniseries
by USA TODAY *bestselling author Michelle Major!*

"I'm going to call my friend who's a nurse in the morning. She's not working in that capacity now, but she grew up in this town. She'll help get you with a good physical therapist."

The warmth she'd seen in his eyes disappeared, and she told herself it shouldn't matter. It was better they remember who they were to each other—people who had a troubled girl in common but nothing more.

She couldn't allow it to be anything more.

"You need a Christmas tree," he said as she started to back away.

"I didn't see any decorations in your house."

He nodded. "Yeah, but Stella made me promise I would at least get a tree."

"I'll consider a tree," Madison told him. It felt like a small concession. "Although I'm not much for Christmas spirit."

"That makes two of us."

Once again, she wasn't sure how to feel about having something in common with Chase.

He cleared his throat. "I have more work to do—meetings and deadlines to reschedule. I can make it back to the bedroom."

"I'll see you tomorrow."

"I'll be here." He laughed without humor. "It's not like I can get anywhere else."

"Good night, Chase."

"Good night, Madison," he answered.

The words felt close to a caress, and she hurried to her bedroom before her knees started to melt.

Don't miss
Starlight and the Christmas Dare *by Michelle Major,*
available December 2022 wherever
Harlequin Special Edition books and ebooks are sold.

Harlequin.com

HARLEQUIN
PLUS

Announcing a **BRAND-NEW** multimedia subscription service for romance fans like you!

Read, Watch and Play.

Experience the easiest way to get the romance content you crave.

Start your **FREE 7 DAY TRIAL** at <u>www.harlequinplus.com/freetrial</u>.

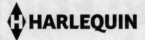 **HARLEQUIN**

Heartfelt or thrilling, passionate or uplifting—Harlequin is more than just happily-ever-after.

With twelve different series to choose from and new books available every month, you are sure to find stories that will move you, uplift you, inspire and delight you.